WINE COUNTRY COURIER
Community Buzz

STOMACH FLU OR MORNING SICKNESS?

We've spotted our friend Mercedes Ashton running in and out of every bathroom from here to Nebraska. And I don't think she was trying to dodge reporters! And to add to the rumor about her being in the family way, it seems our glowing Mercedes is suddenly engaged. To whom? Not to ex-boyfriend Craig, but to longtime best friend Jared Maxwell. So whose baby is it?

Hmmm...? Friends to lovers? Not impossible... just fishy...or shall we say convenient? Being a die-hard romantic myself, I'd love to believe the two have finally fallen madly in love with each other. But the skeptic in me wonders if this isn't just a matter of convenience.

You know what? No matter. The family needs a little diversion from all the hoopla surrounding Spencer Ashton's murder! He certainly had plenty of enemies. Still, it would be nice if we could find out once and for all who was behind the murder....

Dear Reader

Silhouette Desire has a fantastic selection of novels for you this month, starting with our latest DYNASTIES: THE ASHTONS title, *Condition of Marriage* by Emilie Rose. Pregnant by one man...married to another, sounds like another Ashton scandal to me! *USA TODAY* bestselling author Peggy Moreland is back with a brand-new TANNERS OF TEXAS story. In *Tanner Ties,* it's a female Tanner who is looking for answers...and finds romance instead.

Our TEXAS CATTLEMAN'S CLUB: THE SECRET DIARY also continues this month with Brenda Jackson's fabulous *Strictly Confidential Attraction,* the story of a shy secretary who gets the chance to play house with her supersexy boss. Sheri WhiteFeather returns with another sexy Native American hero. You fell for Kyle in Sheri's previous Silhouette Bombshell novel, but just wait until you get to really know him in *Apache Nights.*

Two compelling miniseries also continue this month: Linda Conrad's *Reflected Pleasures,* the second book in THE GYPSY INHERITANCE—a family with a legacy full of surprises. And Bronwyn Jameson's PRINCES OF THE OUTBACK series has its second installment with *The Rich Stranger*—a man who must produce an heir in order to maintain his fortune.

Here's hoping this September's selections give you all the romance, all the drama and all the sensationalism you've come to expect from Silhouette Desire.

Melissa Jeglinski

Melissa Jeglinski
Senior Editor
Silhouette Desire

Please address questions and book requests to:
Silhouette Reader Service
U.S.: 3010 Walden Ave., P.O. Box 1325, Buffalo, NY 14269
Canadian: P.O. Box 609, Fort Erie, Ont. L2A 5X3

CONDITION OF MARRIAGE

Emilie Rose

Published by Silhouette Books

America's Publisher of Contemporary Romance

Special thanks and acknowledgment are given
to Emilie Rose for her contribution to the
DYNASTIES: THE ASHTONS series.

To the ladies of eHarlequin and the Brainstorming
Desirables loop. You are a riot, and I don't know what I'd
do without our Wednesday chats.

 SILHOUETTE BOOKS

ISBN 0-373-76675-0

CONDITION OF MARRIAGE

Visit Silhouette Books at www.eHarlequin.com

Printed in U.S.A.

Books by Emilie Rose

Silhouette Desire

Expecting Brand's Baby #1463
The Cowboy's Baby Bargain #1511
The Cowboy's Million-Dollar Secret #1542
A Passionate Proposal #1578
Forbidden Passion #1624
Breathless Passion #1635
Scandalous Passion #1660
Condition of Marriage #1675

EMILIE ROSE

lives in North Carolina with her college-sweetheart husband and four sons. This bestselling author's love for romance novels developed when she was twelve years old and her mother hid them under sofa cushions each time Emilie entered the room. Emilie grew up riding and showing horses. She's a devoted baseball mom during the season and can usually be found in the bleachers watching one of her sons play. Her hobbies include quilting, cooking (especially cheesecake) and anything cowboy. Her favorite TV shows include Discovery Channel's medical programs, *ER, CSI* and *Boston Public*. Emilie's a country music fan because there's an entire book in nearly every song.

Emilie loves to hear from her readers and can be reached at P.O. Box 20145, Raleigh, NC, 27619 or at www.EmilieRose.com.

THE ASHTONS

Frederick Ashton m Patricia Winston

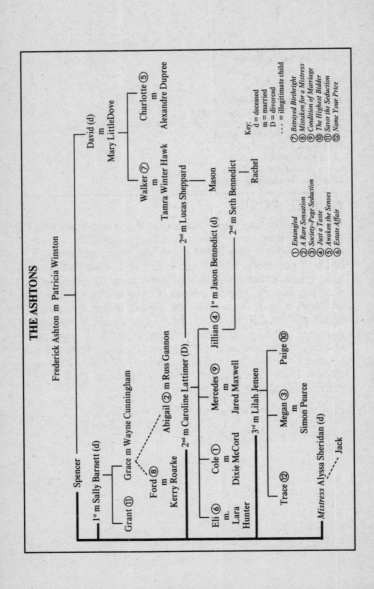

Spencer

Grant ⑪
1ˢᵗ m Sally Barnett (d)

Grace m Wayne Cunningham

Ford ⑧
m
Kerry Roarke

Abigail ② m Russ Gannon

David (d)
m
Mary LittleDove

Walker ⑦
m
Tamra Winter Hawk

Charlotte ⑤
m
Alexandre Dupree

2ⁿᵈ m Caroline Lattimer (D).

Eli ⑥
m.
Lara Hunter

Cole ①
m
Dixie McCord

Mercedes ⑨
m
Jared Maxwell

3ʳᵈ m Lilah Jensen

Jillian ④ 1ˢᵗ m Jason Bennedict (d)

2ⁿᵈ m Lucas Sheppard

Mason

2ⁿᵈ m Seth Bennedict

Rachel

Trace ⑫

Megan ③
m
Simon Pearce

Paige ⑩

Mistress Alyssa Sheridan (d) ----- Jack

Key:
d = deceased
m = married
D = divorced
--- = illegitimate child

① Entangled
② A Rare Sensation
③ Society-Page Seduction
④ Just a Taste
⑤ Awaken the Senses
⑥ Estate Affair
⑦ Betrayed Birthright
⑧ Mistaken for a Mistress
⑨ Condition of Marriage
⑩ The Highest Bidder
⑪ Savor the Seduction
⑫ Name Your Price

Prologue

Spencer Ashton kept his back to the door of his private library long after the maid announced his visitor and departed.

He'd give the no-account farmer his ex-wife had been foolish enough to marry time to see what true class and wealth brought—not that he expected a cellar rat like Lucas Sheppard to have the intelligence or the education to comprehend the value of the original artwork on the walls or the leather-bound first editions on the floor-to-ceiling bookcases.

Let him wait.

"You can ignore me as long as you like, Ashton. I'm not going anywhere."

Cocky bastard. Spencer spun his chair around, but he didn't stand. "To what do I owe the displeasure of your visit, Sheppard? Are you finally willing to concede you can't make a living off that scrap of land Caroline's mother left her?

Perhaps you want to sell it to me after all. Of course, I've lost interest now. My offer will be lower."

The look he sent Sheppard had sent many a wiser man scurrying away. This idiot held his ground and his gaze. "Not at all. I've come to talk to you about the children."

Son of a bitch. He wanted more money to take care of Caroline's brats. "You have thirty seconds. I'm a busy man."

For the first time since his entrance, Sheppard seemed ill at ease, and Spencer enjoyed his discomfort. "I love Eli, Cole, Mercedes and Jillian as if they were my own. I want to adopt them."

Anger burned through Spencer's veins like a lit fuse on dynamite—a short fuse. He might not want the brats underfoot, but they were *his,* by God, and Spencer Ashton never gave up anything unless he had a damned good reason. Making his ex-wife and Sheppard happy wasn't a good reason. "No way in hell."

"Ashton, you haven't seen the children once since you walked out on them three years ago. They need a father."

Spencer laughed. "They're better off without a father than to be saddled with a no-account like you."

Sheppard's nostrils flared, and anger flashed in his eyes. "You self-righteous son of a—"

"You're wasting my time. Remind Caroline that those brats belong to me. She made the deal. I expect her to abide by it."

"Then perhaps you ought to visit your children or at least send birthday cards."

Spencer rose slowly, menacingly. He parked his fists on the desk and leaned forward. "Don't cross me, Sheppard. If you do I'll sue for custody and take the children."

A bluff, but then a wise man always knew when to bluff. Caroline's own father had taught him that much—right before Spencer had beaten him at his own game. Spencer now owned everything that had once been Lattimer's, and he no longer had to endure Caroline or her whiny children to have it.

"You wouldn't stand a chance of winning a custody suit. You took almost everything Caroline owned and abandoned those kids when you divorced her."

"Ah, but lawyers can be so time-consuming and expensive, and I can afford the best. I'm sure you'd hate for your precious Caroline to have to sell Louret Vineyards to pay her legal fees. Do you think my mousy ex-wife would still love you if you cost her what little she has left?"

His barb hit the target. Spencer savored the defeat creeping over Sheppard's features.

"You are one coldhearted son of a bitch, Ashton." He stormed out.

Spencer sat back in his leather desk chair, steepled his fingers and smiled. "You don't know the half of it, Sheppard. But you will."

One

"**S**tomach flu?" Jared Maxwell offered Mercedes Ashton a clean, damp washcloth.

"I wish." Mercedes released her hold on the toilet bowl, accepted the cloth and let Jared pull her to her feet in the tiny bathroom of his cottage. She swayed.

Jared cupped her elbows, steadying her. Her pale skin, combined with her unusual silence during dinner and the tension pleating her brow and pulling her generous mouth, concerned him. "Then it must be my cooking."

She offered a weak smile at his attempted humor. "Your cooking was excellent as usual. Why else would I appear on your doorstep every Wednesday night for the past eleven years?"

Puzzled, he leaned against the doorjamb. "Then what's going on?"

Mercedes pulled free and turned to wash her face and

hands. When she finished she fussed with her hair, trying to smooth the curly caramel strands back into the twist pinned at the back of her head. Mercedes usually let her hair down as soon as she entered his cottage, both literally and figuratively, but she hadn't tonight. She straightened the blouse of the suit she'd worn to work at the family winery earlier today. She wouldn't meet his gaze in the mirror, and Jared suspected she was stalling. Why? They had no secrets.

The sight of her trembling hands sent a sense of foreboding through him. What could she be afraid to tell him?

Finally she sighed, straightened her shoulders and turned. She avoided his gaze and focused on a spot beyond his shoulder. "Would you mind if I left a little early tonight?"

"Yes, I'd mind. Mercedes, I can't help, if you won't tell me what's wrong."

"You can't fix this." The agony in her voice and in her sea-green eyes pierced him.

"Did you ever listen to me when I said that to you?" Mercedes had stood by him through the death of his wife and child and his subsequent bout with alcohol abuse. She'd been his wife's best friend. Now she was his.

She winced. "No."

He tucked a stray curl behind her ear. "It's my turn to be the hero. Give me a chance."

She pressed her lips together, but not before he noticed a telling quiver. "Can we go back into the den?"

"Whatever you want."

"I want to go home." The irritable tone was completely out of character for his calm, controlled friend, but then she'd been fidgety for most of the evening.

He forced a smile despite his growing concern. "Except that."

She led the way back to the den, settled in her usual spot

in the corner of the sofa, but she didn't kick off her shoes, tuck her feet beside her or pull the afghan over her legs the way she usually did. Her stiff posture, tightly closed eyes and clenched fists spoke of an inner struggle. "Craig's gone."

"Good riddance." Jared wished back the words when surprise and hurt flashed in her eyes. He held up a hand to stop her protest. "I don't mean to be unsympathetic, but you know I never liked the guy. He wasn't good enough for you. None of the losers you seem to favor ever are. Frankly, Mercedes, your taste in men sucks."

A derisive smile curved her lips. "Don't hold back."

He shrugged. Mercedes was the only person he trusted enough to be one hundred percent honest with. Make that ninety-nine percent. He had one secret he'd never share. "If you try to tell me you're broken-hearted over his departure I'm not going to believe you. You weren't in love with him."

She sighed and pressed her fingertips to her temple. "No. No I wasn't, and I won't miss him, but…"

The mantel clock ticked off thirty seconds. He waited for her to complete her sentence. When she didn't, he prompted, "Did you have an argument?"

She grimaced. "Yes and no."

That certainly didn't sound like Mercedes's usual decisiveness. "Care to elaborate?"

Was that fear in her eyes? Adrenaline raced through his veins. He slid to the edge of his leather club chair. "Did the bastard hurt you?"

"Not physically. He—" She broke off and clutched her hands until her knuckles turned white. Her troubled gaze locked with his and she worried her bottom lip with her teeth. "He asked me to get an abortion."

For one stunned moment Jared thought he'd misunderstood, *prayed* he'd misheard, and then he hurt, as if a million shards of glass had exploded inside him. His throat closed up. His heart pounded like a jackhammer. His stomach clenched and his skin turned cold—as cold as that of his dead son. He gulped on the bile rising in his throat. "You're pregnant."

Mercedes chewed her lip and eyed him uneasily. "Yes. I didn't want to tell you until…until I decided what I'm going to do."

He was dying inside. He wanted to storm out of the house and keep running until the pain subsided. But he couldn't. Mercedes had led him out of the hell his life had become six years ago. He owed her. If not for her, he'd be buried beside his wife and child—if they'd ever found his body.

"You didn't tell me because you thought it would remind me of Chloe and Dylan." His flat voice broke when he said his son's name. Pain filled his chest and crept up his throat, choking him.

A tear streaked over the dusting of freckles on Mercedes's pale cheek and into the corner of her wide mouth. "Yes. I'm sorry."

For the first time since he'd given up alcohol five years ago, he wanted—no, he *needed*—a drink and the numbness it would bring. He fought to shove down his emotions and conquer the demons inside. "Have you made a decision?"

Again she hesitated. "I'm keeping my baby."

He drew in a ragged breath, stood and crossed to the mantel. Bracing both hands on the wide wooden slab, he fought to inhale but his constricted chest made that almost impossible.

"I'm not my father, Jared. I can't pretend this child never existed. My baby may not have been planned, but it will *never* feel unwanted or unloved." The painful neglect she'd suffered at Spencer Ashton's hands laced her tone with need, but conviction strengthened her voice.

He couldn't do it. He couldn't stand by and watch Mercedes's belly swell as the child inside developed. He couldn't risk seeing the baby move beneath her skin or coming to anticipate its birth. Caring for someone and losing them wasn't something he wanted to risk again. If anything went wrong he'd never survive the devastation a second time. If not for Mercedes, he never would have survived losing Chloe and Dylan.

A swish of fabric preceded the warmth of her hand on his stiff spine. "I didn't want to hurt you."

"Is he going to marry you?" He struggled to squeeze words past the noose around his neck.

Her bitter laugh held no mirth. "No. He claims the baby isn't his, and he says there is no way he'll tie himself down to someone else's brat."

Stunned, he faced her. "You weren't seeing anyone else."

Her lips turned downward in a cynical grimace. "I see you at least once a week, Jared, sometimes more, and then there are the occasional weekends we go away to B&Bs together. Craig thinks the baby is yours."

His jaw dropped. His brain scrambled to make sense of the insane allegation. At the same time mental and physical barriers slammed into place. His muscles tensed and his skin drew tight as if trying to armor himself against the pain he knew would follow.

"Those are business trips. We've never slept together. For God's sake, we don't have that kind of relationship."

"I know that and you know that, but Craig doesn't believe it. Or maybe he's using our relationship as an excuse to escape responsibility. Anyway, he's willing to pay for an abortion, but otherwise he wants nothing to do with this pregnancy or the baby. He accepted a job with a firm in southern California to reinforce his point in case I missed it."

He shoved a hand through his hair and hoped her brothers, Eli and Cole, and sister, Jillian, could be there for her during and after the pregnancy because he couldn't. "What did your family say?"

She ducked her head and fussed with one pearl earring. "I haven't told them, and I'm not going to. Not yet."

He didn't try to hide his surprise and confusion. Mercedes worked with her siblings daily. This wasn't something she could hide. "Why not?"

The pain in her eyes hit him square in the gut. "What do you want me to tell them? Guess what? I'm stupid enough to get pregnant by a man just like my father? And just like my father Craig's going to abandon his child?"

Pain stabbed his left temple. "Mercedes—"

She wrung her hands and paced the floor. "My family is going through hell right now. The press is crucifying us over the recent revelation that my parents' marriage was never legal. Instead of focusing on the winery's new marketing campaign that Cole and I sweated over, the press watches our every move like vultures hovering over roadkill waiting for a whiff of scandal. They want to see the factions of the Ashton family battle—preferably until blood is drawn."

He couldn't argue with that. The press had grown increasingly bloodthirsty since Spencer's murder in May. Jared's throat closed up. "How far along are you?"

"Eight weeks. I've done a home pregnancy test, but I haven't seen a doctor yet for fear of the press finding out. I know I can't keep the secret indefinitely, but as soon as Spencer's murderer is found the press will leave us alone."

"You won't have long before you start to show. A couple of months at the most. And you need to see a doctor now—before it's too late." Chloe had lost babies at eight- and ten-weeks pregnant.

"I know. I remember, too." She laid a hand over his forearm. His muscles knotted beneath her touch. Why did her fingers feel so hot? Was it because he was so cold?

If Mercedes remembered how much he'd loved his wife, how excited he'd been over the fact that their third pregnancy had nearly reached term after two earlier, devastating miscarriages, how could she forget he'd almost killed himself in his grief over losing his wife and son less than a month before the baby was due? Because he'd never told her how close he'd come to taking that final step. Mercedes had no respect for weak men, and he'd been weak.

"A baby will mess up your well-ordered life." *And his.*

She lifted her chin. "I know, and I don't care. Jared, I value your friendship more than anything. Please don't let this pregnancy come between us."

"Your family will help you," he said through clenched teeth.

She flinched, paled and pressed a hand to her chest. "And you won't?"

"I can't."

Seconds ticked past. "Do we have to give up our dinners?"

The tremor in her voice squeezed the breath from his lungs. Pushing her away was killing him, but his sanity—*his survival*—depended on putting some distance between them. "Not yet."

But soon. He didn't voice the words, but they hovered in the air between them.

He'd hurt her. Her pain was plain to see in the darkening of her eyes, in the strain in her features and in her quivering lips, but she nodded and stepped away. "I understand. All I ask is that you keep my secret until I'm ready to tell my family."

"You're making a mistake."

"No, my mistake was accidentally getting pregnant by a

man I knew I could never love." She gathered her bag and her blazer and paused by the door. "But, Jared, life goes on and you have to play the cards you're dealt. You can still win the game with a bad hand, you know."

How many times had she said those words to him back in the dark days when his life had been a black gaping void?

He cared more about Mercedes than anyone else. How could he let her down?

How could he not?

If anyone asked her—and they hadn't—Mercedes would swear that her family was coming apart at the seams, unraveling because of the threads Spencer Ashton pulled from the grave. Damn her father for his lying, conniving, narcissistic ways.

She swallowed her anger, her ever-present nausea and a rising panic over the loss of control in her own well-organized life and entered the bistro. She spotted her youngest—*as far as she knew*—half sister, Paige, across the dining room and waved away the hostess. Weaving her way through the tables, Mercedes scanned the patrons, on the alert for tabloid reporters the way a small animal would be for signs of a predator ready to leap from the brush and attack.

She probably should have refused the luncheon invitation rather than risk becoming ill in public and feeding the rampant speculation about the Ashton family saga. The last thing her family needed right now was more grief, and that's all a premature leak about her pregnancy would cause at this point. But she hadn't wanted to hurt Paige's feelings.

She'd get her life back together by herself—*thank you very much*—and then she'd tell them. She didn't doubt they'd rally around and support her…. Well, Mercedes conceded with an inward wince, she didn't doubt it much. Given the recent eye-opener that her father had illegitimate offspring all over the place—including her and her siblings—she couldn't be sure her family wouldn't frown on her decision to continue this pregnancy. But continue it she would, because everything happened for a reason, and this baby had a purpose, as yet untold, for being here. And then there was the fact that she was thirty-three, didn't believe love existed except for a rare few instances and didn't plan to marry. This could be her only shot at motherhood. Even though she liked children, she'd never planned to have any of her own, but from the moment she'd discovered she was pregnant she'd wanted this baby.

Paige smiled, rose and took Mercedes's hand. "Thank you for coming."

"Your request sounded urgent."

"Yes. I wanted to ask…" Paige's gaze skidded away and then returned. "How are you? I heard you'd broken up with your boyfriend."

Mercedes sighed, sat and reached for a bread stick. Craig had been gone for weeks, and she really didn't want to talk about him, but she could handle chitchat as long as her stomach cooperated. Paige would eventually get to the real reason for the impromptu Thursday luncheon invitation. Besides, if Mercedes hadn't accepted Paige's invitation she would have sat in her office and worried about how she was going to cope with the pregnancy without Jared in her corner. She counted on his strength and his friendship, probably more than she should. He'd been a fixture in her life ever since he'd met and married her best friend. As it was, she'd barely slept last night because worry had kept her up and pacing the floor.

"Yes, Craig is history, but I'm okay with that. Dare I ask how you heard? I didn't think his departure had made the tabloids yet." The bread stick tasted like sand. Great, even her taste buds had gone on strike.

"Kerry, my father's—*our* father's—assistant, mentioned it. I met Craig when you brought him to the fund-raiser back in February. He's quite attractive."

"And charming, funny and a great date, but he was also shallow, disloyal and not a guy you'd want to grow old with." A lot like her father actually. Definitely not a man she could love. That, of course, was one of her criteria for dating.

Paige blinked at Mercedes's bluntness, but the waitress arrived before she could reply. Mercedes ordered a ginger ale and the blandest pasta on the menu and prayed her stomach would behave.

She liked Paige. Her half sister reminded her of how young, naive and excited she'd been about life eleven years ago. It seemed like an eon since she'd been a twenty-two-year-old college student savoring the last days of freedom before joining the family business. A smile tugged at her lips. She had a permanent reminder of those fun, uninhibited days before she'd buckled down, hidden beneath her slim, pin-striped skirt.

Of course, Paige already worked for Ashton Estate Wineries, so maybe her half sister's carefree college days were already over.

"No wine?" Paige asked.

"No. I left a mountain of work waiting on my desk. I need to keep a clear head." How long would it take for people to pick up on the fact that the marketing and PR director of Louret Winery and Vineyard had given up drinking the company product?

Excitement sparkled in Paige's hazel eyes. She leaned forward. "Have you heard about the bachelorette auction fundraiser we're hosting at Ashton Estates next month? Perhaps you could place yourself up for bid and find Mr. Right?"

Mercedes grimaced. Somehow she didn't think a pregnant woman whose stomach revolted unpredictably would be a great prize. "I think I'll pass."

Besides, she never dated a man who didn't have at least six characteristics from the "Twenty-five Ways To Tell Your Man's a Loser" list she and her friend Dixie had developed during their last year of college after both of them had their hearts severely dented. Screening the potential bidders for loser-list qualities was impossible; therefore, putting herself up for bid was not an option.

Everywhere Mercedes looked, the marriages around her ended in heartache. After years of infidelity, her father had abandoned her mother to marry his secretary. He hadn't been faithful to that wife, Paige's mother, either. Her sister, Jillian's, first marriage had been disastrous. Jared and Chloe's marriage had been magical, but when Chloe and the baby she carried had died in a car crash Jared had lost himself in grief. She knew his heart still belonged to Chloe and he'd never love another.

Mercedes doubted she was strong enough to endure the kind of pain loving and losing inevitably brought. Why risk it? To keep from falling into the love trap, she only dated men she could never fall in love with—men who didn't have the power to hurt her.

The waitress arrived with their meals, breaking into her dark thoughts. Mercedes sipped her ginger ale, nibbled her penne and hoped her meal would stay down. "How is your mother holding up?"

Paige's eyes darkened. "Dad was… He was such a dynamic person. It will be hard to go on without him. We're all struggling with our grief."

Finding out Spencer had fathered another illegitimate child while married to Paige's mother probably hadn't helped the grieving process. And the recent disclosure that Spencer had abandoned a wife and two children before marrying Mercedes's mother hadn't exactly been a eulogizing moment, either. Had Spencer Ashton loved anyone but himself? Poor Paige seemed to have no clue what a selfish bastard their father had been.

Mercedes's stomach started to churn. She reached for her ginger ale. How many half siblings did she have anyway? She could name six, but were there others? Would the publicity over the unsettled estate bring more relatives out of the woodwork? She'd certainly been taken aback by the value of Spencer's estate, and she wouldn't be surprised if others wanted a slice of the Ashton pie.

At the close of the meal Paige set down her fork and bent to withdraw several folded tabloids from the leather bag at her feet. She laid them on the table. "Actually, this is why I asked you to join me for lunch. Have you seen the latest?"

"No, and I'm not sure I want to." But Mercedes scanned the headlines, finding more of the same speculation and allegations that had hovered over Napa Valley like a fog for the past few months.

Will the Ashtons Become the Next Hatfield-McCoy Family Feud?

Will They or Won't They Contest the Will?

Will the Bastard Branch Harvest Their Father's Estate?

Mercedes pushed the papers away. None of these were as creative as her all-time favorite. Ashtons Aim Their Corks at Each Other. The reporter had gone on to dub the Ashton debacle as the Battle of the Vineyards. He'd compared the Ashton Estate Winery to Goliath and Louret's smaller boutique winery to David. It saddened Mercedes to think what the personal costs might be before the situation could be resolved.

Her father's death had turned his children into adversaries whose every move had become fodder for the tabloids. Mercedes felt like a movie star with all the paparazzi but none of the perks. Each intrusive headline reinforced her decision to keep her pregnancy under wraps for as long as possible. Maybe she could run off to work in France for a year with her half brother Mason and return after her baby's birth. She sighed and nixed the idea. Her family needed her here in Napa. And Jared…she'd yet to figure out what she was going to do about Jared, but she had no intention of losing his friendship. Besides, running never solved anything.

Paige tucked the tabloids back into her bag. "We have to do something. Our families and our businesses are suffering."

Mercedes nodded. "I agree, but I don't know what we can do to turn off the publicity machine."

Paige hesitated a moment. "Could you speak to Eli and ask him not to contest the will?"

Ah…the true reason for the lunch invitation emerged. "My brother is doing what he feels is right. The land on which the Ashton Estate Winery sits, as well as the Ashton-Lattimer Corporation should rightfully belong to my mother since they were *her* father's properties. Since Spencer never bothered to divorce his first wife, my parents' marriage wasn't legal, either. Any divorce settlement he received from the dissolution of their marriage shouldn't be legal. As much as I wish it were different, there just isn't a simple way to heal this breach."

Paige gestured toward the papers. "I'm sure we can quietly come to an understanding instead of having our laundry aired in a public forum."

If only it was that easy to erase pain, outrage and betrayal. "Paige, I'm all for making peace between our families. I'm not sure it's possible, but I'll do what I can."

* * *

"You weren't leaving without me, were you?" Mercedes called through her open car window as she parked in the shade beside Jared's SUV.

The muscles in Jared's strong jaw bunched, and his thick, straight brows lowered. A cool breeze blowing off the lake ruffled his dark hair, and the midafternoon sun glinted off a scattering of silver strands at his temples. He wore khaki pants and her favorite polo shirt—the one that made his eyes seem impossibly blue.

He shoved his bag in the back of his vehicle. "I didn't think you'd want to go."

Mercedes swung her legs from the car and closed the door. "I've gone with you on every scouting trip for potential bed and breakfast purchases. Why wouldn't I go this time?"

He hesitated. "Are you feeling up to it?"

At the moment, yes. Five minutes from now was another story, but she kept that tidbit to herself. In the wee hours of her second sleepless night since telling Jared about her predicament, she'd decided that once the shock of her pregnancy wore off, their relationship would return to normal. She didn't want to lose her best friend, and she was convinced the way to attain that goal was to maintain the status quo. If that meant ignoring her pregnancy for the time being, then she would.

Mercedes slung the strap of her purse over her shoulder. "I'm up to it. If you don't want my opinion, then you're going to have to have the guts to say so."

He swiped a hand over the five-o'clock shadow covering the lower half of his face. "I value your input."

"Then let me get my bag and we'll go. To be honest, I'm looking forward to getting out of Napa Valley for the weekend. I feel like a bug under a microscope."

She hustled to the trunk of her sports car as quickly as she could in her heels. She'd rushed straight from the winery without stopping by her apartment to change out of her work clothes because she'd been afraid Jared would take off without her. He had a tendency to go off and brood when he was upset. And her news had upset him.

Jared beat her to the rear of the car and reached past her to retrieve her overnight bag. Their hands met on the handle of the case. A tingle traveled up Mercedes's arm. Jared's chest brushed her back. His heat penetrated through her thin rayon suit, and his larger frame seemed to enfold hers as he reached around her for her bag. The hair on her nape moved beneath the whisper of his breath, and an unwelcome sensation stirred in her abdomen.

Surprised, she turned her head toward his. Scant inches separated their mouths. His minty breath caressed her lips, and his dark-blue gaze fastened on hers. He blinked and blanked his emotions. He'd done that with other people before, but she couldn't remember Jared ever blocking her out. That answered one question. *If* he felt the strange connection between them he planned to ignore it.

Good plan. One she heartily endorsed.

He frowned. "You shouldn't be lifting heavy items."

Surprised by the sudden dryness of her mouth, she wet her lips. "I packed light. We're only going to be gone overnight."

A tight smile slanted his mouth. "I've seen the way you pack. Light has nothing to do with it. I have your bag. Let go."

She released the handle and surreptitiously wiped her tingling palm on her hip while he carried her overnight case to the back of his SUV. Mercedes took her time securing her vehicle although her little car would be perfectly safe here beside the guest cottage on the grounds of the bed and breakfast inn Jared and Chloe had bought during the first year of their marriage. She tried to regulate her choppy breathing and calm her jangled nerves.

What was going on here? Jared was her *friend*. She'd never had a sexual reaction to him before. His heart belonged to Chloe—always had, always would. He was off-limits.

So how could she explain her damp palms and racing pulse?

Damned pregnancy hormones. Her breasts were so tender even the brush of her bra and blouse aroused her.

"Ready?" he asked.

"Yes. You know I wouldn't have to pack so much if you'd tell me where we're going once in a while instead of always trying to surprise me." She climbed into the passenger seat and buckled up as she'd done dozens of times before, but today was different. She could feel Jared trying to put distance between them, and she didn't intend to let him.

"You like my surprises. We're headed for the Sierra Nevadas."

Surprised, she lifted her brows. "That's more than an hour away."

She waved to Mr. and Mrs. White, the managers of Jared's B&B, as Jared drove past the Victorian main house. Mercedes had hired the couple six years ago when Jared, lost in his grief over Chloe and Dylan, had been unable to keep up with his duties as host. She'd expected the position to be temporary, but Jared hadn't wanted to run the inn without Chloe. He'd become a silent owner. In recent years he'd turned his hotel management background into collecting financially struggling inns across the wine country and turning them into profitable enterprises. She helped him hire the couples to manage the inns.

She shifted in her seat and found his gaze on her. He nodded toward the innkeepers. "You did well in choosing the Whites. I never would have hired them."

"No, you would have sold the place along with Chloe's and your dream. She loved this house with all its gables, fancy trim and deep porches."

A sad smile touched his lips. "So did you. I'm not sure which of you loved it more."

He was right. At the time, Mercedes had been a tad envious that Chloe had not only snagged the perfect man, one who adored her and didn't register on the jerk-o-meter, but also because her friend would get to live in this dreamy, romantic home with its delicate gingerbread trim and octagonal turrets.

Mercedes shook off the uncomfortable memories. Okay, so she didn't actually believe in romance, but she loved this house, and Jared…Jared was a true gem. She couldn't lose his friendship.

"Tell me what makes the B&B we're visiting today special enough to add it to your collection."

He shrugged. "It's a family place."

She raised her brows. Until recently Jared had avoided B&Bs that catered to families with young children. Did this mean he was healing? "Instead of a romantic couples' retreat or spa theme? That is a departure for you."

"The property is 160 acres in the California Gold country north of Yosemite. There are twenty rooms inside the inn itself and thirty cabins on the grounds. The current owners offer hiking, fishing, cross-country skiing and white-water rafting along with the usual tourist attractions."

She nodded. "I can see the appeal. They offer all of the popular hobbies, but it's larger than your other properties and quite a bit farther away—out of the wine country, in fact. Will we go rafting this weekend?"

"I might. You won't."

She sat back in surprise. "I beg your pardon?"

EMILIE ROSE   27

"It's too risky." He cut her a look as he turned onto the highway. "You need to think about the baby."

She understood his concerns. Chloe had lost two pregnancies early on, but she wasn't her petite, delicate friend. "Jared, I'm not fragile."

His fingers tightened on the wheel until his knuckles whitened. "You have no way of knowing that."

"I hike, raft and kayak with you on a regular basis. I'm in good shape."

His gaze raked over her. Every fine hair on her body rose at his thorough perusal—as did her nipples. Horrified by her body's reaction, she folded her arms and prayed he hadn't noticed, but with the snugger fit of her suit jacket over her pregnancy-swollen breasts, her distended flesh would be hard to miss.

Maybe she could blame her absurd reaction on the amount of time that had passed since she'd been intimate with a man. Her last encounter had been the time she'd conceived. Before that…well, she and Craig had been on the verge of ending their relationship, so there hadn't been much contact. As Jared had pointed out, she didn't love Craig. He was a convenient and charming escort who knew how to work a room at the numerous functions her job required her to attend, but he had an annoying tendency to flirt with her female friends, which made them all uncomfortable. It was amazing what a woman would tolerate when she didn't believe in love.

Sayonara sex and a birth-control failure had resulted in the baby she carried.

Jared's lips tightened. "Yes, but now that you're pregnant your balance will be affected."

"I haven't gained an ounce and my equilibrium is just fine, thank you."

"You've lost weight, Mercedes. Conserve your energy."

"You're not going to leave me in my room. For heaven's

sake, Jared, it's not like I'm insisting on going hot-air ballooning or bungee jumping with you this time."

"Good thing. I wouldn't allow it."

He wouldn't allow it! Anger stirred. "I have two older, overprotective brothers—thank you very much. I don't need another one."

His jaw muscles bunched. "I'm not your brother."

"No kidding." That had never been more apparent than now when her rebellious body seemed determined to misbehave.

"All I'm asking is that you keep your feet on terra firma until after your baby is born."

As if she'd do anything to put her baby in jeopardy, Mercedes silently fumed.

They lapsed into a long, tense, uncomfortable silence—something that had never happened on their road trips before. Saddened, Mercedes closed her eyes and leaned back against the headrest. In addition to the rampant hormones, her pregnancy left her exhausted much of the time. Her limbs felt weighted.

Jared's cologne filled her senses and she smiled, remembering the day ten years ago when she and Chloe had picked it out. The moment Mercedes had smelled the subtle blend of citrus, cedar and wood smoke she'd known this brand was perfect for an outdoorsman like Jared. He'd worn it ever since.

"Watch out." Jared's sharp warning jolted Mercedes back to consciousness. The heavy application of the vehicle's brakes threw her against the protective arm Jared had extended in front of her. Adrenaline surged through her system.

"What happened?" She blinked groggily.

"A deer ran in front of the car." He slowly lowered his arm, but the imprint of his touch remained on her breasts. He examined her with a concerned gaze. "Are you okay? I didn't hurt you?"

"I'm fine. Sorry, I must have dozed off. Are we there yet?"

"The inn should be around the next bend."

"Good, because I need the ladies' room in the worst kind of way." And she needed to get her pregnancy hormones under control, because she'd enjoyed Jared's touch in a most *un*-friendly way.

Two

Responding to a knock, Jared opened the connecting door between his room and Mercedes's. His jaw dropped.

He'd seen Mercedes in her plain black one-piece swimsuit dozens of times before, but she'd never filled it out quite the way she did today. Or if she had, he hadn't noticed. He shouldn't be noticing now, but her substantially expanded cleavage was hard to overlook.

He swiped one hand over his face and struggled to make sense of the words Mercedes had spoken. "You're going where?"

She looked at him as if he'd lost his mind, and maybe he had, and then she folded her arms, which did not help the situation. The move lifted her creamy skin even higher out of the suit.

"I'm going swimming. The brochure says the pool is heated. I need to work out the kinks from the drive. Are you going to join me after your usual walk around the grounds or corner the owners to go over the inn's financial statement?"

She knew him too well, but he hoped like hell that she didn't realize that the sight of her standing there with her curly hair falling over her pale, *exposed* chest had reminded him that he was very much a man. Disgusted by his base response, he shoved his fists in his pockets to hide his condition and studied the ornate washstand beside the door. "I'll walk the grounds and then take a look at the books."

His libido had been dormant since Chloe's death, and he didn't know what to make of the sudden awakening of his hormones. He didn't dare join Mercedes in the pool. "Stay out of the hot tub and sauna. Elevated temperatures are dangerous for the baby."

She took a sharp angry breath and nearly spilled from her suit. Sensing her impending explosion, he stepped away from the door, but the heat settling low in his groin and pulsing in unison with the throb in his temple wasn't as easy to evade.

Bad move. Increasing the distance between them brought her sleekly muscled, bare legs into the picture. Her weight loss combined with her increased bust measurement made her look like a centerfold model, and his body reacted predictably.

"I won't keep you from your swim." And then he wisely shut the door and strategically retreated into the hall.

He descended the stairs and let himself out onto the front veranda. With any luck the cool evening breeze would clear the inappropriate thoughts from his head. In the past two days his relationship with Mercedes had gone from easy and relaxed to decidedly uncomfortable.

Every mental corner he turned reminded him of Chloe, the excitement of each pregnancy, the crushing pain of the miscarriages and the devastating blow of her death. He couldn't go through that wringer again with Mercedes. He cared too much, and the thought of losing her put a knot in his gut that no amount of antacid could dissolve as the half-eaten roll in his pocket attested. No, he didn't love Mercedes in the same way he'd loved his wife, but Mercedes had become an important part of his life. Too important.

He never should have let himself care about her. Caring brought pain. What kind of fool was he that he hadn't learned that lesson by now? He'd lost his family—not to death but to a gaping chasm of hostility—and then his wife and son, and soon he'd have to let Mercedes go.

But how could he turn her away? She was as much a part of his life as the sunrise. He counted on her friendship and her business acumen. Thanks to Mercedes he'd made a success of the inns.

Thirty minutes later he came around the back corner of the inn and found Mercedes swimming laps in the pool. She spotted him, stopped at the edge of the pool and waved him over.

"Come in. The water's great, and before you ask, the pool is in good condition. I checked."

They had a well-established routine when investigating potential properties. Examining the pool always fell into Mercedes's jurisdiction. He crossed the deck, stopping a yard away. The weight of the water had straightened her corkscrew curls into a sheet of café-au-lait colored satin that reached just beyond her shoulders. Water droplets glistened on her skin and eyelashes. The buoyancy of the water lifted her breasts with each wave.

His mouth turned as dry as the desert. He'd seen her this way more times than he could count, but his new awareness of her as a woman disturbed him. "I should go over the books tonight."

"Your loss." She lifted an arm, drew back and splashed a

cascade of water over him. Typical Mercedes maneuver—at least it was typical when she was away from the pressure of her job with the family winery. There she seemed to be more driven than anyone he knew except himself—as tightly wound as the hair she kept pinned back on her head. If he hadn't been so distracted, he would have anticipated her horseplay.

He chuckled. "Witch."

"You know where to find me if you change your mind." With that parting salvo she ducked under the water and headed for the opposite end of the pool.

He watched her lithe form for a few seconds and then wiped the water from his face and turned away from the inn to continue his tour of the grounds. Desiring a few minutes to get his thoughts back on track before confronting the owners and their ledgers, he headed deeper into the aspen trees surrounding the cabins instead of returning to the primary structure.

The shadows and solitude of the woodland suited his mood. After Chloe's death he'd wasted a year camping, staring at the bottom of a whiskey bottle and avoiding people and life in general. Mercedes had been relentless in her quest to drag him back to the land of the living. She'd tried coddling and then bullying him out of his misery. He'd resisted her every step of the way.

One night while camping on the northern California coast he'd decided he couldn't go on without his wife and child. He'd stumbled drunkenly to the edge of the cliff and looked down at the waves breaking on the jagged rocks below. He'd been on the verge of taking that final step when Mercedes had called him back.

No, she hadn't physically been with him on the cliffs that night, but he'd heard her just the same and known that if he ended his agony, hers would begin. She'd miss him, mourn him in a way his own family wouldn't. His father had disowned him when he'd left the family hotel chain to marry Chloe and open the bed and breakfast. His two older brothers, caught in the middle of the feud with his father, rarely called.

Mercedes was the only one he had left, and he'd promised Chloe he'd look out for her. In the years since Chloe's death Mercedes had become his family, and she'd dragged him into hers. But soon Mercedes would have a baby, a family of her own, and he didn't know if he could bear to be around her and be reminded of what he'd lost and what he would never have.

It was a classic case of he couldn't live with her, but he seriously feared he couldn't live without her.

What in the hell was he going to do?

"What's your vote?" Jared asked as he joined Mercedes at the table in the sunny breakfast room of the inn.

Mercedes took in the gleam of Jared's freshly shaven face, his broad shoulders beneath a powder-blue polo shirt, and the jeans riding low on his hips. His cologne filled her senses and her stomach flip-flopped. She broke eye contact and glanced out at the amazing view of the meadow. He was too handsome for his own good. Her resistance was abnormally low, and her hormones were out of control.

"I vote yes, and if you buy the inn, I'm going to beg you to let me manage it for the next year or so." She could love it here away from the stress, the press and her complicated family situation. She hadn't been queasy once since they'd arrived last night. Her appetite had returned this morning with a vengeance, and she'd consumed an embarrassing amount of food. Despite that, the contents of Jared's plate made her mouth water. She reached out and swiped a grape.

He nudged the dish in her direction. "Hibernating is my thing, not yours. You love your job and family."

She shrugged. "You're right, but it's a tempting thought."

His expression turned serious. "I want you to see a doctor."

Her appetite vanished. "I will."

The determined set of his mouth suggested arguing might be a waste of time. "I mean today. I have a repeat customer who's an obstetrician. I've called Dr. Evans, and she's agreed to work you into her Saturday clinic. She'll be discreet."

Speechless, Mercedes stared at him. "We haven't finished inspecting the inn."

"I've seen enough to know I'm interested in sending up a building inspector and making an offer. The owners will fax me the rest of the information. If we leave after breakfast we can make it to Sacramento in time for your appointment. I want to make sure you're in good hands."

Before he dumped her. He didn't say it, but she received his message loud and clear. Anger percolated in her bloodstream. He wasn't going to shake her off that easily.

"Jared, I know you mean well, but making my doctor's appointment isn't your decision."

He covered her hand with his and his somber gaze locked with hers. "Do this for me. Please."

His concern defused her anger. The warmth of his skin permeated hers and her mouth moistened. That shimmery feeling she'd experienced when their hands had met on her suitcase handle multiplied ten-fold, traveled up her arm and descended through her torso to settle in the pit of her stomach and below.

She knew she should argue, assert her independence, but she couldn't seem to find the words to debate. "Fine, but if I'm going, you have to come with me."

He rocked back in his chair. "I'll drop you off."

"No deal."

"Mercedes—"

"Jared...I'm scared, okay? I need you there." She hated to admit it, but she remembered what Chloe had gone through, too. She'd shared the joy and the pain, and she'd accompanied her friend to doctor's appointments on the few times Jared couldn't get away. She'd been the one holding Chloe's hand the day the doctor couldn't find the second baby's heartbeat, and Mercedes didn't want to be alone if the news wasn't good. No, this pregnancy hadn't been planned, but she already loved her baby, and she was excited about the future they could have together.

Her baby. She pressed a hand over her belly.

Jared observed the gesture with a jaw set and blanked eyes. What she was asking wouldn't be easy for him. "I'll wait in the reception area."

Jared jerked to a stop inside the doctor's private office. His throat constricted and his pulse pounded in his ears. "What's wrong?"

Mercedes, already seated in one of the two chairs in front of the doctor's desk, looked surprised to see him. "Nothing...that I know of."

"Then why did you send for me?" How could he put distance between them if she kept dragging him into her pregnancy?

A frown pleated her brows. "I didn't."

A trickle of fear slithered down his spine. Why would the nurse bring him back here if there wasn't something wrong? His stomach clenched. Bile burned his throat. Memories of the past descended on him like a cold, lead blanket. He opened his mouth to insist that he shouldn't be here, but the worry clouding Mercedes's eyes made him hesitate.

She clenched the wooden arms of her chair with a white-knuckled grip. "Do you think there's a problem with my baby and they didn't want to tell me while I was alone?"

Before he could answer, Dr. Evans entered and waved him toward a chair. "Please have a seat, Jared."

Jared battled between his need to leave and his duty to Mercedes. Duty won. Could he be strong for her? Yes, dammit, he could. He owed her that much. He sat down beside Mercedes and took her cool hand in his.

The doctor, a middle-aged woman who'd been one of Jared and Chloe's first customers, settled behind her desk and smiled. "I'm happy to report that everything about this pregnancy looks good, excellent, in fact."

Air rushed from Jared's lungs in a relieved gush, but concern remained. "But…" he prompted.

She only hesitated a moment. "I've been a visitor to the Lakeside B&B for many years, so I know what a difficult past you've had, Jared. I also know the Ashtons are particularly newsworthy at the moment. As I told you on the phone, I can promise my staff will be discreet, but I can't speak for the patients in my waiting room. We whisked Mercedes through as quickly as possible, but…"

She shrugged and opened Mercedes's file. "You never know what the press will dig up. Now, the good news is Mercedes's health couldn't be better, and with the fetal heartbeat in its current range, the chance of miscarriage is less than ten percent." She paused and looked directly at Jared. "Your baby appears to be as healthy as can be. You should be proud parents in early to mid-April."

His baby? He recoiled. Where the hell did Dr. Evans get that idea? His gaze jerked to Mercedes.

She bit her lip, hesitancy and confusion plain on her face. If Mercedes hadn't misinformed the doctor, then who had?

Oh, hell, Jared realized the doctor must have misinterpreted what he'd said when he called her at home last night to request an appointment for Mercedes. Should he correct her? Or should he keep his mouth shut? If the people they'd encountered this morning thought he was the father, then they wouldn't look further. On the other hand, a mystery always drew interest, speculation and in the Ashtons' case, reporters.

He squeezed Mercedes's hand and silently urged her to follow his lead. "Good. What kinds of precautions should Mercedes be taking?"

Mercedes blinked. Questions filled her eyes, but she remained silent.

"Mercedes asked about exercise, and I've instructed her to use common sense and avoid risky sports, but I don't see a problem with hiking, biking, swimming activities in which she already participates on a regular basis. And you can resume sexual relations at any time. Mercedes said it had been a while."

His gaze ricocheted from Mercedes's stunned, red face to the doctor and back again. His mouth dried and his pulse missed a few beats before racing ahead at Daytona 500 speeds.

Him.

Mercedes.

Sex.

He'd never connected the three, and he didn't want to now, but fire raced through his bloodstream and need—shocking, unacceptable, and damned urgent—throbbed in his groin.

All he could think while the doctor rattled on about prenatal vitamins and diet was he had to get the hell out of here.

"Did I miss something back there?" Mercedes asked when the silence of the drive got to her. Tension filled the cab of the SUV like a dense, impenetrable San Francisco fog.

"I could have sworn I intentionally left the *father* part of the patient information form blank."

Jared's grip tightened on the steering wheel. "The doctor might have misinterpreted something I said."

Mercedes noticed the nerve ticking in Jared's jaw. "What *exactly* did you say, Jared?"

He didn't take his eyes off the road ahead. "I said, 'Someone very special to me is pregnant.'"

Her heart quickened, which was stupid, of course, because she knew her relationship with Jared was special—just not special in *that* way. She cringed. When the doctor had asked how long since she'd last had sex, Mercedes hadn't hesitated before answering. She hadn't known the doctor would leap to such an erroneous conclusion or mention Mercedes's celibate status to Jared.

Sexual relations with Jared. An image of hot, sweaty bodies sliding against each other flashed on her mind's movie screen, and surprisingly, her reaction was far from repulsed. In fact, her stomach fluttered and filled with heat—a totally taboo response.

Damned pregnancy hormones. "That's all you said?"

"That's it."

"I'll correct Dr. Evans on my next visit. I'm going to continue seeing her until closer to my due date, and then she'll refer me to a practice near home. I stand a better chance of avoiding the press that way."

He hesitated and his brows lowered. "What's the point of correcting her unless you want Craig's family history included in the paperwork?"

In a perfect world Mercedes would have the complete medical history of her baby's father, but this wasn't a perfect world. "I don't want to call Craig to get his history. I know enough. I made sure he was healthy before I slept with him. His parents are in their late seventies. He often complained that they were disgustingly hale and hearty and had no time for their only child. His father plays golf several times a week and his mother is on the seniors' tennis team."

Her baby would inherit good genes from his father's side. Apparently, that was all Craig intended to contribute.

Jared nodded. "Then let it ride. What harm can it do?"

"It's dishonest. I'd rather not start my baby's life with a lie. My father built a life based on lies, and look how that's come back to haunt us."

He sent her a glance so filled with understanding that warmth settled low in her belly and tears pricked Mercedes's eyes. "As you said, you're not your father."

"No, but I don't think lying is ever the best option, and unless you want to come to every appointment with me and play the devoted daddy-to-be, then I need to straighten this out."

Jared's shoulders tensed and his jaw knotted. He couldn't withdraw any further without getting out of the car. "I'll call her office first thing Monday morning."

Mercedes sighed and leaned her head against the headrest. Jared was determined to establish a barrier between them. How could she stop him?

Life as she knew it was about to change. Yawning, Mercedes pulled into her assigned parking space outside the apartment building and turned off the car's engine.

For starters, she'd have to move. There wasn't room in her studio apartment for a baby. And she'd have to get a new car. Her tiny two-seater wouldn't hold a car seat. She yawned and stretched. Maybe after a nap she wouldn't be too exhausted to plan for her future.

She unlocked the apartment door, stepped inside and froze. Craig Bradford reclined on her sofa. Her exhaustion vanished. "What are you doing here?" she said.

Craig rose, smiling his most practiced smile and assuming the posture that she'd learned meant he wanted something. She'd once found him attractive with his dark-blond hair and blue eyes and let's-have-fun attitude. Now she saw a man so much like her father that she couldn't believe she'd ever become involved with him. Stupid, stupid, stupid. And now she carried his baby.

"How did you get in?"

He produced a key from his pocket and held it up.

Mercedes silently cursed. She and Craig had never lived together, but she had loaned him a key once because she couldn't leave work to retrieve the cell phone he'd left in her apartment. He must have had a copy made. She crossed the room and reached for it.

He lifted it out of range. "I made a mistake. I love you and I want to marry you."

Shock stopped her midstride. "What?"

"I was scared. Mercedes, love, I've never thought twice about being a father. You surprised me, that's all. But now I'm ready."

She could see the lie in his eyes. "You don't love me, Craig. You love you. That makes one of us. What do you want?"

"I want us to spend the rest of our lives together."

"The rest of our lives." Skeptical, she folded her arms. "Just you and me, for richer and poorer, in sickness and in health, keeping only unto each other for as long as we both shall live?"

She glimpsed a touch of panic before his gaze danced away and then returned. His throat worked as he swallowed. "Yeah."

Mercedes laughed in disbelief. Not only did Craig avoid illness like the plague and rely heavily on his creature comforts, his blatant flirting with her female friends had almost cost her those friendships. He didn't know the first thing about fidelity—the kind of love that Jared had shared with Chloe. Mercedes wouldn't settle for less. Not that she believed she'd ever find it. And she certainly wasn't looking.

"Come on, Mercedes, let's run off to Vegas. When we get back we'll build a nice house using the money you're going to inherit from Ashton's estate and play mom and dad with style."

Did his voice break over the word dad? "Craig, I'm not inheriting any money, and I don't want to marry you."

"The papers are full of the news that your father was loaded, and your brother is contesting the will. All of your father's property will revert to your mother's children. That means one quarter of that estate belongs to you, sweetie."

Money. This was all about money? Why was she surprised? "Nothing has been decided about the estate, and I'm still not going to marry you."

Craig was an ambitious salesman dedicated to making acquaintances of the rich, famous and influential. For a while Mercedes had been happy to make those introductions because his smooth-talking and pleasant persona also helped her expand Louret's client base.

His expression turned petulant. "You will or I'll sue for joint custody of that little Ashton heir you're carrying."

Mercedes's knees collapsed as reality slapped her. She sank into her wicker rocking chair. Craig was more like her father than she'd thought. He didn't want her or her baby. He wanted to get his hands on the Ashton money, and he'd use this child as a pawn to do so. *Not as long as she was breathing.*

"What happened to your claim that this baby wasn't yours?"

He didn't try to varnish the truth with charm now. Bitterness flattened his lips. "I told you. I was upset."

"You ordered me to get an abortion, Craig."

Panic crossed his features. "You didn't, did you?"

It would be so easy to lie—but unfortunately, also so easy to disprove. "No. I told you I wouldn't."

His insincere, ingratiating smile returned. "Good. Let's get married."

"No."

"Mercedes," he sing-songed. "Come on. We're good together."

Correction. They were *okay* together. No stars, no fireworks, no weak knees. They'd been better at increasing each other's client base than as a romantic couple. "Give up, Craig. It isn't going to happen."

"Do you really want your child to be a bastard?"

He didn't have to add *like you.* Mercedes immediately relived the shock and shame she'd experienced eight months ago when she'd discovered her parents' marriage had never been legal. And now, she was repeating her father's mistakes. But she wouldn't let her child suffer. "Better a bastard than a pawn in a nasty divorce."

Anger flashed in his eyes. He stalked to the door, but paused with his hand on the knob and turned to glare at her. "Then you'll hear from my lawyer."

The door slammed behind him, jarring the picture of her family from the wall. The glass inside the frame shattered on impact with the floor. Mercedes feared her well-ordered life was about to do the same.

Her stomach revolted. She bolted to the bathroom and lost her lunch. When the retching subsided she sank to the floor, clutched her middle and sagged against the bathroom cabinet. What was she going to do? She couldn't let Craig get his hands on this baby. She'd experienced life with a father who, when he wasn't ignoring you, treated you like a necessary evil. My God, Spencer hadn't even recognized Jillian, *his own daughter,* at the reception the Ashton Estates Winery, her father's other company, had held earlier this year. Mercedes rubbed her tummy. Her child would never know the pain of being discarded and forgotten.

Panic clawed at her insides. She couldn't think for the pounding in her head. Jared would know what to do. He excelled at assessing a situation and formulating a logical plan of action.

She staggered to the phone and dialed his number. A sob skipped up her throat when his deep baritone answered. "Jared, I need you."

Mercedes opened the door before Jared could knock. She looked near shock. Her pupils were dilated and her skin waxy. "What am I going to do?"

He cupped her elbow and guided her back into her den. "First, you're going to sit down, and then I'm going to make you a cup of your favorite tea."

Mercedes wrapped herself in the quilt Chloe had sewn for her and curled in her rocking chair. Satisfied that she wasn't going to pass out at his feet, Jared crossed to her kitchen and prepared the tea. He visited often enough that he knew where Mercedes kept everything, including her favorite mug.

"Tell me exactly what Bradford said," he called over his shoulder.

"He read about Eli contesting the will in the papers. Craig said he wants us to run off to Vegas and then come back and build a house using the money I'll inherit. If I refuse he'll sue for custody."

Jared shoved the mug into her hands, pinched the bridge of his nose and tried to think of a better way to offset Bradford's claim—a way that didn't knot his intestines or make him crave a shot of mind-numbing whiskey. He drew a blank. The insane idea that had forced itself into his mind on the drive over refused to be supplanted by a saner one.

A sense of inevitability closed in, wedging him between the proverbial rock and hard place. He exhaled slowly. "Tell him the baby is mine."

Mercedes clutched her mug and gaped at him. Some color returned to her cheeks, but the worry darkening her sea green eyes to jade didn't fade. "We can't do that."

"We're only confirming what he already believes. Hell, it was his idea."

"But it's a lie," she protested.

Yes, dammit, and he hated lying and liars which was one of the reasons he'd never liked Bradford, the smooth-talking, opportunistic bastard. But what other option did they have to keep the parasite from following through with his threat? If Mercedes felt like a bug under a microscope now, it would be nothing compared to the media frenzy if Craig sold his story to the highest bidder. She and her baby would become the next bone for the press dogs to fight over. The added stress wouldn't be healthy for her or the pregnancy.

He crossed the room to stand before her. "Which is worse, us lying about your baby's paternity or Bradford lying about suddenly loving you and using the child you're carrying to get his hands on the Ashton estate?"

"You're arguing semantics."

An urge to smooth her tangled curls blindsided Jared. He shoved his fists in his pockets. "Do you have a better idea?"

"No, I don't, but I can't let him have this baby, Jared. He'd be no better a father than Spencer, and no child deserves a father who makes her feel like an unwanted possession that he can't wait to shed." She set the mug on the end table and hugged the quilt tighter. "What if he demands a DNA test?"

"You can refuse to have the testing done until after the baby is born. Prenatal DNA testing is risky for the fetus. No court would require it. Do you think he'll hang around that long once he realizes that Spencer's estate isn't likely to be settled for years?"

"Honestly, no. I think Craig wants a fast buck and the publicity the Ashton name brings. He's a salesman. That kind of name recognition would help his career. But Jared, there's something else to consider." She hesitated and his nerves stretched taut. "My family didn't like Craig, and they'd never expect me to marry him… But they love you."

The quiet statement hit him with the force of a battering ram to the gut. He clenched his teeth and abruptly turned toward the window. His mind, his heart and soul screamed *no,* but he knew which path he had to take—the one he'd sworn never to travel again. Still, he couldn't force the words past his paralyzed vocal cords.

He heard Mercedes sigh. "I'll hire a lawyer and try to get Craig declared an unfit father. I have plenty of friends who can testify that he made passes at them while we were supposedly an exclusive couple, and the fact that he bolted as soon as I told him I was pregnant should carry some weight. God, I wish I'd kept the check he threw at me when he told me to get an abortion, but I was so angry I shredded it and flushed it. I'll just have to hope what I have is enough."

The doubt in her voice ripped him open. He set his jaw. Forcing one tight, aching muscle and then another to move, he turned until his gaze met hers. "We'll get married."

She gasped and her knuckles clutching the quilt whitened. "No. *No,*" she repeated with more strength. "I won't let you do that."

"You'll have my name and my protection. We'll present a

united front—not just the two of us, but your entire family will stand behind us."

Sad shadows filled her eyes. "I won't let you deface your memories of Chloe that way."

Chloe. She'd loved Mercedes like a sister from the time the two girls had met back in grade school. Chloe, his generous, loving wife, would want him to help—no matter what the cost. "Mercedes, it's your only option if you want to avoid a long, public legal battle."

Mercedes rose, and the quilt slid to the floor. Tension strained her features as she crossed the room. The shadows beneath her eyes looked darker than they had an hour ago. "You are my best friend and I love you for what you're trying to do, but I won't let you make this sacrifice."

He cupped her shoulders to prevent the hug he suspected was coming, and her curls teased the backs of his hands. He couldn't handle close contact now when his nerves were on edge and his body seemed to have its own agenda. "I wouldn't have made it through the last six years if not for the sacrifices you've made for me."

She lifted her hand to cradle his jaw. Mercedes could scale a cliff and negotiate Class IV white water with ease. She'd done both with him countless times. He'd known she was in great shape, but he'd never experienced the strength and warmth of her muscles shifting beneath his fingers. A surge of testosterone pumped into his blood, heading toward an unacceptable target zone. He lowered his hands and shoved them into his pockets, but the heat of her satiny skin lingered in his palms.

Clearing his throat, he put the width of the room between them. "Once Bradford slinks back under his rock we'll quietly separate and divorce. We're looking at a couple of years. Three at the most."

Doubt clouded her eyes. "What would we tell my family?"

"If you want to keep the truth out of the press then we tell everyone the same story. We've been friends for years. They'll buy that we've become...lovers." Saying the word sent another shot of heat through his system. Fast on the heels of heat came pain. He'd never love another woman like he'd loved Chloe. He wouldn't—*couldn't*—risk it. "When we end it we'll tell them we were better friends than lovers."

"Would we be...lovers?"

Her quiet, hesitant question shook him like an earthquake. "No. It'll be a marriage in name only."

Hugging herself, she paced to the window. "I'm not comfortable with lying to my family."

"Do you want to risk the truth getting out? We can't guarantee that family conversations won't be overheard. Servants talk and they've been known to sell secrets. Any hint that we're not a happy couple will strengthen Bradford's claim by making it appear that we've concocted this story to deliberately deceive him and exclude him from his child's life."

"We *have* concocted this story to keep him away from his baby." Her shoulders slumped and she gave a resigned sigh. "If we do this, then where would we live? This place is too small, and so is your cottage."

"We'll have to buy a house."

Worry pleated her brow. "What about us?"

"What about us?"

Her eyes beseeched his. "Jared, can you promise me a marriage won't ruin our friendship?"

His chest constricted and it hurt to breathe. Everything had changed the moment she told him she was pregnant. Life came with no guarantees, but right now, Mercedes needed assurance more than she needed additional uncertainties.

"You have my word that I'll stand by you, Mercedes, for as long as I'm able."

And God help him, he'd do whatever it took to keep that vow.

Three

Mercedes faced her mother and sister across her kitchen table on Sunday afternoon. She touched her queasy stomach and prayed this decision wouldn't come back to haunt her.

Setting down her teacup, she folded both hands in her lap to hide their trembling. "Thanks for coming over. I need your help."

"What kind of help?" her sister Jillian asked.

"Planning a wedding."

Her mother's cup rattled on the saucer. "To Craig?"

The dismay her mother couldn't quite conceal brought a sad smile to Mercedes's lips and reaffirmed her decision. Craig was a jerk, and erasing him from her life was the right thing to do for everyone concerned—especially her baby. "No. To Jared."

After a stunned moment of silence, Jillian squealed, jumped to her feet and pulled Mercedes into a bouncing hug. "It's about time you saw the prize right in front of your nose."

Her mother added her own hug and beamed. "Congratulations. You know Lucas and I love Jared as if he were one of our own. What did you have in mind? A spring wedding, or perhaps summer?"

"Actually, we'd like to get married right away." Mercedes licked her dry lips and took a deep breath. Her stomach churned. "I'm pregnant, but I'd like to keep that among the three of us for the time being."

Slack-jawed, Jillian sank back into her chair. Mercedes could see the questions in her sister's eyes, but she hoped Jillian wouldn't ask them, because Mercedes didn't know if she could look her in the face and tell a bold-faced lie. None of them needed to check their Day Planners to know that Craig had been gone little more than a month, and here Mercedes was pregnant and planning to marry another man.

Mercedes resettled in her seat and forged ahead. "We'd prefer a small, intimate wedding with only the immediate family present, and since Jared's in the middle of negotiating the purchase of the inn we visited yesterday, we're going to have to postpone the honeymoon."

Her mother eased gracefully back into her chair. "Perhaps we could hold the ceremony in my garden?"

Perfect. The eight-foot-high stone wall surrounding her mother's garden should keep out the press. "If you don't mind?"

"Of course not. The garden was always your favorite spot. You could say your vows in front of the fountain. Did you have a date in mind?"

Mercedes's heart raced. She couldn't believe she was actually going to go through with this. "As soon as we can make the arrangements. Tomorrow is Labor Day. The courthouse will be closed for the holiday. Jared and I will apply for the marriage license on Tuesday morning as soon as they open. Do you think we could arrange it by Saturday afternoon?"

"I could call the minister who married Seth and me to see if he's available, if you like," Jillian offered hesitantly.

"That would be great." Mercedes tried to smile, but her numb lips wouldn't cooperate.

"We could shop for a dress tomorrow," her sister added with a little more enthusiasm. "Everything will be on sale."

Mercedes swallowed. She hadn't thought about a wedding dress. If she didn't buy something, her family would ask questions she didn't want to answer. "I don't want anything fancy to remind Jared of his wedding to Chloe."

Her mother patted her hand. "His marriage to Chloe was a long time ago, and she's been gone six years. He'd want you to have your dream wedding, but if you'd prefer a simple ceremony, then you shall have one."

"Thank you. I'll prepare a press release, but I'd rather nothing leak out until after the ceremony. I'm worried that Craig might make trouble. We didn't part on the best of terms, and he's come sniffing around now that he believes I'll inherit some of Spencer's money."

Her mother nodded with a tightening of her lips. "We'll hire extra security. Will Jared's father and brothers be attending?"

Yet another component Mercedes hadn't considered. "I don't know. There's still a lot of tension between them, but I'll ask Jared if he wants to invite them."

Her mother nodded again. "His family will be our family now. They're welcome to stay here at The Vines. I'll call and make the offer myself, if you'd like."

The lie grew more convoluted by the minute. Her family loved Jared and would willingly embrace his family. They'd all be hurt when the truth eventually came out.

So Mercedes lifted her chin. She'd have to do whatever she could to keep the truth from surfacing. Once Craig was no longer a threat, she and Jared would part as he suggested, claiming they were better friends than lovers.

Lovers. Her skin flushed hot and she couldn't seem to catch her breath. For the first time in her pregnancy, Mercedes thought she might faint. She and her husband could not, *would not* become intimate. She wouldn't betray Chloe's memory that way. Nor did she want to risk falling for the one man who had the power to breach the walls she'd built around her heart.

"Absolutely stunning," Caroline Ashton whispered in a tear-laden voice as she tucked the last of Mercedes's curls in place with a pearl-tipped hairpin. She stepped back so Mercedes could view her handiwork in her mother's bedroom mirror.

Mercedes swallowed to ease the tightness in her throat and met her mother's watery gaze in the mirror. This wasn't the wedding day Mercedes had pictured for herself, but then she'd never pictured herself ever trusting a man enough to marry him. "Jillian has incredible taste. The dress is lovely."

Given the circumstances of her hasty marriage, Mercedes had refused to wear bridal white. Nor had she wanted to look young or innocent since at thirty-three she was neither, and ruffles and flounces had never been her style. She'd suggested a simple, elegant suit, but her sister had refused to let her be so practical or staid.

Jillian had dragged her from shop to shop until they'd discovered this lingerie-style slip dress. The delicate beading edging the bodice, hem and the thin shoulder straps sparkled subtly on the antiqued ivory silk when Mercedes moved. The fabric skimmed her figure before flaring slightly around her ankles. The elegant and romantic wedding dress made Mercedes feel beautiful despite a huge case of nerves and tremendous reservations about the ceremony ahead.

She smoothed her hands over her hips and took a quick peek in the mirror to assure herself that the reason behind the rushed ceremony didn't show.

Jared didn't deserve this. Every step of the way had been painful for him—not that he'd uttered one word of complaint. He'd said nothing at the county clerk's office when he'd had to produce Chloe's death certificate as part of the application for a marriage license, but Mercedes's heart had ached for him. His fingers had lingered for a split second longer than necessary on the page, sweeping over Chloe's name as if he were saying goodbye again. His silence, the muscle ticking in his jaw and the rigid set of his shoulders had revealed far more about his pain than mere words could say.

If Jillian, their witness, had noticed Jared's reluctance, she hadn't mentioned it.

"Ready?" Jillian asked, draping a sheer shimmering silk stole over Mercedes's shoulders.

"As ready as I'll ever be." Mercedes quivered inside.

"I'll get our bouquets from the kitchen." Jillian slipped out the door.

As elegant and stylish as ever, Caroline Lattimer Ashton Sheppard dabbed a tear with a lace handkerchief. Mercedes would never understand how her mother could take a second chance on love after the way Spencer Ashton had hurt and betrayed her, but in her mother's case it had paid off. Lucas Sheppard, Mercedes's stepfather, treated Caroline like a queen. Their deep, abiding love was evident in every glance and touch.

Men like Lucas and Jared were few and far between. Seth, Jillian's new husband, looked as if he might be one of that rare breed as well. He'd certainly made her sister very happy in the past four months. Mercedes sighed and adjusted a curl. Why was it that the men worth a second glance were already taken?

Caroline's reflection joined Mercedes's in the mirror. "It's almost time to start. I'll get Lucas."

Mercedes turned, caught her mother's hand and squeezed her fingers. "Mom, thank you for putting this together so quickly. The garden looks like something from a fairy tale."

If her mother had guessed Mercedes wasn't in love with her groom-to-be she hadn't said so. Caroline had gone out of her way to turn the garden into the ideal location for a romantic fantasy wedding. Even the climbing roses lining the high white stone wall of her mother's private garden had cooperated by producing a fresh set of fragrant blossoms. Additional potted plants had been placed in every available niche and along the brick walk from the back door of The Vines to the fountain in front of which she and Jared would exchange their vows.

"Just be happy." Her mother kissed her cheek and left Mercedes alone in the room with her suffocating doubts.

Panic clawed at her stomach. What if this marriage was a horrible mistake? Others would be hurt. She pressed a hand below her navel and thought of her painful relationship with Spencer. Could she inflict that on an innocent child? No, she wouldn't make her child beg for crumbs of attention. She'd give her child enough love to make up for denying her a father. And maybe, just maybe, Jared would be a father figure for her baby once the shock of the situation wore off.

The bedroom door opened and Lucas Sheppard stepped inside. He'd married her mother when Mercedes was six and had brought a sense of normalcy back to their lives after her father's abrupt departure. Still handsome, tall and fit at sixty, Lucas walked with a slight limp—a remnant from the years of hard work in the vineyard. He'd combed every gray hair in place.

She smiled. "You look dashing in your tuxedo."

"And you're going to knock Jared right out of his shoes."

If only that were true. Mercedes blinked away the rogue thought. She wasn't out to seduce her husband-to-be.

Lucas took her hand and met her gaze. A solemn expression replaced the usual twinkle in his blue eyes. "This is the part where I'm supposed to remind you that it's not too late to change your mind. This baby is nothing we can't handle."

Her mother had asked if she could share the pregnancy news with Lucas, and Mercedes had agreed. Emotion welled in Mercedes's throat. She smiled and brushed a piece of lint from his shoulder. "And that's just one of the reasons I love you. No matter what kind of situation I found myself in, you were always there to guide me. You know I couldn't have dreamed up a more perfect father if I'd tried. I'm lucky to have you in my life, Lucas Sheppard, and my baby will be even luckier to have you as a grandfather."

Tears dampened his eyes, and Mercedes's own eyes burned. He yanked her into a big bear hug, and then drew back abruptly. "Don't want to muss the dress."

"*You* can muss me anytime." She straightened his bow tie and kissed his cheek.

"Ready to get this show on the road? Some of that stuff the caterers brought in looks mighty tasty."

Mercedes's stomach pitched at the thought of food. She took a deep breath and pasted a smile on her face. A simple ceremony and two gold bands could put her friendship with Jared on the line. He deserved the same opportunity to escape that Lucas had offered her.

"Could you give me a minute?"

* * *

A cold calm settled over Jared as the clock inched toward noon. Moving forward meant leaving the past behind. He hadn't expected it to be so difficult.

Marrying a woman who wasn't Chloe seemed like a betrayal. But abandoning Mercedes to her opportunistic ex was no less disloyal. The past, his life with Chloe, was over. Handing over her death certificate had made that clear. Mercedes and her baby deserved a future without Bradford mucking it up.

Through the French door leading from the library to the garden patio Jared watched his sisters-in-law, niece and nephews and his older brother, Ethan, take their seats inside the walled garden with Mercedes's siblings. Behind him, his oldest brother and best man, Nate, lounged on the sofa, talking quietly with the minister.

Jared was surprised his brothers had come. His father hadn't. But then his father had never forgiven him for putting Chloe's dream of running a bed and breakfast inn ahead of family obligations. When Jared had refused to return to the fold after Chloe's death, the gap had widened even more. Both of his brothers were dutifully employed by Maxwell Hotels, Incorporated. They seemed happy enough under their father's controlling thumb. Jared hadn't been.

As the third son he was supposed to toe the line and do what he was told without question, but he'd needed to forge his own path, to succeed on his own merit and not just be the old man's puppet. And he had succeeded—albeit on a different path and a larger scale than he'd originally planned. He offered couples who had the desire but lacked the capital the opportunity to live their dreams of running cozy B&Bs. In a way he was keeping Chloe's dream alive, but from a safe distance.

A tap on the door sent Jared's stomach plunging toward

his polished shoes. *Time's up.* He flexed his tense shoulders as the minister rose to answer the summons.

Nate joined Jared by the French door. "I wish you'd let Ethan and me throw a bachelor party for you or at least let us take you out, booze you up and raise a little hell."

His brothers didn't know about Jared's bout with alcohol abuse. Only Mercedes knew.

"Mercedes and I wanted to avoid the publicity." And it wasn't as if he was saying goodbye to his freedom for the rest of his life. He'd done that when he'd married Chloe.

Looking decidedly uncomfortable, the minister cleared his throat. "Mercedes would like a moment alone with Jared."

Jared's heart slammed against his chest. Did she have cold feet? Didn't she realize this was the only way to protect her name and her baby? Surely she hadn't decided to acquiesce to Bradford's demands. Jared fisted his hands. God help Bradford if he dared to show up today because—

The door opened farther, framing Mercedes in the dark wooden portal like a portrait and choking Jared off midthought. His jaw and his fingers went lax. She looked…amazing. Beautiful. *Sexy as hell.* Jared sucked a sharp breath and took a mental giant step back. Every speck of moisture in his mouth vanished.

She'd pinned her curls haphazardly on top of her head. Stray ringlets caressed her neck and tumbled to her bare shoulders. Was that her wedding dress or the slip she'd wear underneath the dress? My God, she looked half-naked even though only her shoulders in the floor-length gown were bare. She shifted on her feet and the light reflected off pearls and sequins. Her dress, then, not her slip. Somehow the knowledge didn't lessen the impact.

"Give us a minute," he croaked.

His brother punched his shoulder. Jared peeled his gaze off Mercedes long enough to see Nate's wink, smirk and thumbs-up. Nate didn't know the truth behind the wedding.

Mercedes entered the library, and his brother and the minister exited, closing the door quietly behind them.

Her alluring and exotic scent, so different from Chloe's sweet floral perfume, wrapped around Jared and made him dizzy with an adrenaline rush. "You look incredible, Mercedes."

A smile trembled on her lips. "Thank you. So do you."

She lifted a hand to straighten his tie, something she'd done countless times before, but dropped it before making contact. Her fabric stole fell off her shoulders to drape behind her back. Jared considered yanking it back in place, but he didn't want to risk contact with her velvety skin. Besides, the almost sheer fabric wouldn't hide anything.

Closing her eyes, she took a deep unsteady breath, drawing his eyes to her tantalizing cleavage. Her skin couldn't possibly be as soft as it looked. He tried and failed to stifle the thought. The response rioting through his system was completely inappropriate for a man to feel toward his best friend. He clenched his jaw and fought the unexpected and unwanted need snaking through his veins.

"Mercedes, is everything all right?"

"Yes. I…" She lifted her lids. Worry darkened her eyes to jade and a line formed between her brows. "Jared, I know how hard this must be for you. We don't have to get married. I can find another way to fight Craig."

The knot in his throat thickened. "Is that what you want?"

She hesitated. "I don't want to make your life miserable, and if you want to call this off—"

He laid a finger over her lips. She wasn't having second thoughts, but she thought he was. Mercedes worried about him way too much. She'd pulled him out of despair and along the road to recovery. She'd been the giver in this relationship, and he'd been the taker. It was time he carried his weight. Payback time.

His finger burned. He removed it from her soft mouth and shoved his fist in his pants pocket. His knuckles bumped the coolness of the rings he'd bought for her and reminded him that he was here to protect Mercedes and her baby.

"How could having my best friend as a roommate make me miserable?"

"I don't know. I just thought…" She shrugged, and one pearly strap slipped off her shoulder. The front part of her dress—the bodice or whatever you called it—gaped slightly, but enough to shock him with the knowledge that she wasn't wearing a bra.

He gritted his teeth against a flash fire of desire, abruptly raked the strap back in place with one finger and then he knotted his hands behind his back. He shifted his gaze and battled his renegade thoughts. For crissakes, he didn't need to know the size and shape of Mercedes's breasts or the color of her nipples, but he'd had a glimpse, dammit. A tantalizing, torturing glimpse.

Why had he never noticed the delicacy of her shoulders? Sure, she was lightly muscled from their outdoor adventures, but she was also softly curved and feminine. At five feet six inches, she was just over a half foot shorter than he, and slender and petite. Chloe had been even smaller—so tiny and delicate he'd been afraid she'd break if he ever unleashed his passion.

Mercedes wouldn't break.

The mantel clock struck noon, jarring him from his forbidden thoughts with a swift stab of guilt. "Mercedes, stick with the plan."

She frowned at his abrupt tone. "Are you sure?"

"I'm sure."

"If you change your mind—"

"I won't." He considered pulling her into his arms to reassure her. Hell, they'd hugged before. But with the heat percolating beneath his skin and with the new knowledge that her breasts would fit perfectly in his palms, he didn't dare risk it. Taking her by the elbow, he turned her. In that brief second as he reached past her to open the library door, he battled an almost overwhelming urge to touch his lips to her exposed nape. My God, she smelled good. Too good.

He said a prayer of thanks when he found Nate and the minister waiting anxiously on the other side of the threshold. Their presence prevented him from making a mistake and crossing the line of friendship—a line he had no intention of crossing.

"Meet me at the fountain, Mercedes."

With a hesitant glance over her shoulder, she nodded and headed down the hall. The fabric of her dress molded her curves with a lover's detail to accuracy. There weren't any panty lines under her dress, and she wasn't wearing a bra. For heaven's sake, was she naked beneath that wisp of silk? His pulse drummed louder in his ears. He swallowed hard.

Struggling to breathe, he turned on his heel and marched back to the window. What in the hell was wrong with him? His relationship with Mercedes would not change. They'd share a home, companionship, not a bed or hot, sweaty nights. So why did his mind persist in catapulting him in the wrong direction when his hormones had been happily dormant for six years? Longer, if you counted the months he and Chloe had abstained because of her discomfort during the last half of her pregnancy.

"Are we going to proceed?" the minister asked tentatively.

"Yes." Jared reached for the brass lever handle on the French door and yanked it open. He strode to his assigned place beside the fountain, eager to get the formalities over with and to get Mercedes back into some real clothes. Any of her buttoned-up suits would be preferable to the dress that looked more like an undergarment than a wedding dress.

Nate and the minister caught up with him and flanked him. Jared ignored the wiseass smirk on his brother's face, clasped his hands in front and fixed his gaze on the opposite end of the aisle flanked by guests.

From the corner of the garden a harpist plucked out a tune. The double French doors leading from the main part of the house opened, and Mercedes's oldest brother, Eli, escorted his mother down the flower-lined brick walk. Caroline gave Jared a sweet, welcoming smile, and his belly knotted at the deception. She trusted him with her daughter. He wouldn't let her down.

Rachel, Mercedes's three-year-old niece, came next, scattering rose petals randomly over the bricks. When she reached the end of the aisle she rushed to her daddy, seated in the second row, and climbed in Seth's lap. Jared's heart ached. He'd never have a child wind her arms around his neck and his heart with such devotion.

Unless Mercedes's baby— He slammed the protective barrier back in place. He couldn't afford to love Mercedes's baby. Losing Chloe had been hard, but losing his son had nearly destroyed him. His marriage to Mercedes would end, and she'd move out and take her child with her.

By the time he found his composure and looked up, Jillian had made it halfway down the walk. Her mint-green dress resembled Mercedes's, but it wasn't anywhere near as sexy.

Mercedes stepped into the opening, and the knot in Jared's throat threatened to choke him. My God, she was beautiful.

Sunlight danced on her curls and sparkled on the beads and pearls of her dress. But Mercedes was marrying the wrong man. She deserved one who had a heart instead of a cold hunk of ice in his chest. She deserved a man who could be strong for her no matter what.

He would be strong, dammit. He squared his shoulders and awaited his bride.

On the verge of hyperventilating, Mercedes struggled to regulate her breathing, and then she met Jared's gaze across the garden and forgot about breathing altogether.

The strength in Jared's broad shoulders and in his eyes led her forward as surely as Lucas's firm grip on her elbow as he guided her down the steps and along the brick path. Mercedes's hyperalert senses identified the scents of flowers and her mother's herb garden mingled with the aroma of the candles burning in their glass globes beside the fountain, which gurgled in rhythm with the harpist. A gentle breeze ruffled her hair and caressed her shoulders. The silk of her dress slid over her skin like a lover's touch with every step. Her nipples beaded beneath the cool fabric, and there was nothing she could do to hide the telling reaction.

Not once did her gaze leave Jared's. When she reached the end of the short aisle he extended his hand. This is the right thing to do, his steady dark-blue eyes seemed to tell her. Lucas released her, kissed her cheek and stepped away. Jared took his place. His warm fingers curled around Mercedes's, and a sense of calmness settled over her. Her best friend would become her temporary husband. Their friendship had survived worse things than marriage.

Mercedes had made every effort to ensure this wedding was as different from Jared's first as possible. Chloe had written the vows she and Jared had spoken. Her friend had also insisted on a soprano soloist, twelve attendants to waltz down the cathedral aisle, hundreds of guests and custom-made wedding bands. Mercedes had requested simple elegance, and her mother and Jillian had provided exactly that.

The minister began the traditional service Mercedes had heard dozens of times before. The familiar words soothed her tangled nerves. She'd asked for a plain wedding band, but when she looked down at the engagement ring and wedding band set Jared eased onto her finger, she gasped. An emerald-cut diamond winked in the sunlight. The gold bands of the two rings fit together so perfectly that either would look incomplete without the other.

Jared repeated his vows in a firm and sure voice.

Mercedes's voice trembled and so did her fingers when she slid a wide gold band over Jared's knuckle. And then his hands, as warm and solid as a sun-baked rock, cradled hers and calmed her. Right or wrong, the deed was done. She'd married her best friend.

The minister closed his Bible and beamed. "Jared, you may kiss your bride."

Mercedes's heart stumbled then raced. Her shocked gaze jerked to Jared's. How had she forgotten this part? Duty and resolve filled his blue eyes, firmed his square chin. His hands curved over her bare shoulders, and each of his fingers spread a lavalike trail of heat over her body. She dampened her lips. His eyes tracked the movement. She thought she saw a flare of something besides surprise in the split second before he bent his head, but he lowered his lids before she could identify the emotion.

They'd shared numerous hugs and friendly kisses on the cheek, but she couldn't remember their lips ever touching. She barely had a split second to register that Jared had a really great mouth—a chiseled vee on top and lushly curved on the bottom—before his warm, firm mouth settled over hers. And then Mercedes's world went topsy-turvy, as if she'd been swept overboard by the swing of a sailboat boom.

Her eyes slammed shut, and she inhaled sharply through her nose. Jared's woodsy cologne filled her senses, and her head spun as if she'd been tumbled into the water and didn't know which direction led to the surface. Her muscles weakened and her knees buckled. She clutched the lapels of his jacket to keep from sinking to the ground at his feet. Jared's arm banded around her waist, pulling her flush against his lean, hard body. Hot. So hot. She gasped, and his mouth opened over hers. The flick of his tongue on her bottom lip struck her with the charge of a lightning bolt, and then he tasted her. A sip. A silken swipe.

She couldn't help but taste him back. Delicious. Jared. Familiar and yet so spicy and scrumptious she couldn't get enough.

Her hands slid up his neck to tangle in the springy, short hair on his nape. His palms eased down over the slick fabric of her dress to cover her bottom with a blanket of heat. A thick, insistent ridge pressed her belly and melted her bones.

A spattering of applause and laughter penetrated the sensual fog. Jared abruptly broke the kiss and stepped back. Mercedes stared at him in shock. He looked as stunned as she.

"Ladies and gentlemen, may I present Mr. and Mrs. Jared Maxwell." The minister's pronouncement reminded Mercedes of their audience.

She blinked and pasted on what she hoped looked like a blissful bride's smile, but her mind tumbled in chaos.

What was she going to do? She had the hots for her husband.

Four

The urge to run, to put some distance between him and Mercedes hit Jared hard. The wedding kiss had blindsided him. Shaken him. Scared the hell out of him because it made him feel too much.

And that hadn't been the end of it. The reception afterward had been sheer torture.

This marriage was temporary, a favor for a friend. End of story. If he let it become more... He ground his teeth. He wouldn't.

He unlocked the cottage door and shoved it open. A rustle of movement in the shrubbery followed by the reflection of light off a camera lens caught his attention. Damn. Reporters. Though everything in him shouted *distance,* Jared swept Mercedes up in his arms.

She gasped, stiffened and squirmed and kicked her feet. He tightened his arms and struggled to hold on to the slippery, silk-clad bundle in a wedding dress.

"Hold still before I drop you," he whispered against her ear.

"What are you doing?"

"Paparazzi at nine o'clock. I'm carrying you over the threshold." He tried his best to block out her warmth and the exotic scent of her.

She stopped wiggling and wound her arms around his neck. "Already? But Cole isn't sending out the press release until tomorrow."

Jared stepped inside and kicked the door closed. He lowered her feet to the floor and stepped away as soon as she found her balance. Her body heat clung to him even after he put several yards between them. Making his way around the interior of the cottage, he closed the blinds and curtains, sealing out intrusive eyes and turning the room into an intimate, shadow-filled cave. When the last window in the main room had been covered, he ran out of excuses to avoid looking at her.

He snapped on a lamp. "I've cleaned out the second bedroom for you."

Her brows dipped. "Where did you move your office?"

"Loft."

Mercedes frowned at the darkened balcony area overlooking the sitting area of the cottage. The jackhammering of her heart almost drowned out the rustle of her gown and the tap of her heels on the hardwood floor as she moved farther into the room.

"Jared, that space was never intended to be used for anything other than a child's sleeping area. You'll be cramped, and the head clearance is low. There's definitely not room for the two of us to plot out a marketing campaign for the Meadowview Inn if you buy it."

Mercedes had volunteered her advertising expertise when he and Chloe bought the first inn. She'd continued to help him with each subsequent purchase. Because of her contributions his business had gone from one struggling inn to a string of eight flourishing inns, but proximity would be a problem unless he got his head straightened out.

He shoved a hand through his hair. Where would he go? Climbing? Hiking? Rafting? The cabin. Yeah, Mercedes didn't know about his cabin. "Would you prefer to sleep up there? There's not much privacy, and it will be hard to keep up the appearance of happy newlyweds if everyone knows we have separate bedrooms."

She frowned, removed and folded the filmy stole and draped it over the back of the sofa. "I guess you're right. I'm sorry to displace you. As soon as we find a house you'll have your own office again. In the meantime, we'll have to plot our strategies down here."

They'd agreed to buy a home since neither the cottage nor her apartment was large enough for two, let alone three who needed separate bedrooms. He hadn't wanted to be around while her pregnancy advanced, but with the tight housing market in Napa Valley he could be looking at months of being trapped in the guest cottage with Mercedes and her developing baby before they found a house. A duplex would be better. She could live on one side and he could be on the other. He made a mental note to contact a real estate agent Monday morning.

He ran a finger under his collar and loosened the tie that had tried to choke him for the better part of the afternoon. And then he turned on another lamp, but it did nothing to alleviate the intimate atmosphere. "I also cleared out most of the bathroom cabinet for you."

Having only one bathroom sandwiched between the two bedrooms hadn't been an issue before since he lived alone and didn't entertain, but then the cottage had never seemed this small and cramped, either.

He'd survive the shared quarters, but he didn't expect it to be easy. His office location wasn't going to be the main problem. The resurgence of his libido was. His resurrected hormones reminded him that Mercedes would be naked in his shower.

Wet with his water.

Slick with his soap.

He swiped a hand over his jaw and vowed to get out of here as soon as the reporter outside left. The knotted muscles in his shoulders protested when he glanced at his watch and mentally calculated how long it would take him to pack and load his hiking gear into his SUV. He could be at the cabin by midnight.

"Thank you, Jared. I appreciate everything you're doing. This is above and beyond the call of friendship." So formal and stilted, nothing like best friends. Or husband and wife. Mercedes looked as uncomfortable as he felt. And then he noticed the pallor of her skin and the pleat between her brows— a sure sign she had one of her tension headaches brewing.

She worked too hard. The only time he saw evidence of the carefree college girl Chloe had described was when he and Mercedes went on prospective-inn-buying trips. When they checked out the inns, they also checked out the available tourist activities. If he put Mercedes in a raft on the river, she forgot all about the pressures of the family winery. She probably wanted to get out of Napa as much as he did, but he needed time away from Mercedes to regain his equilibrium, not time alone with her. There would be no honeymoon during this temporary marriage.

He headed for the door. "I'll get your luggage and bring in the picnic basket your mother sent with us. You didn't eat much at the reception. You need to eat to keep up your strength. Take a hot shower, if you want. By the time you get out, I'll have something pulled together for dinner."

And maybe the reporter would be gone, and the reluctant bridegroom could take off for Yosemite.

"Jared…" Mercedes hesitated, biting her lip, and then she took an unsteady breath. "I need help getting out of this gown."

His insides clenched like an angry fist. Mercedes slowly turned to reveal dozens of tiny, satin-covered buttons running from her shoulder blades to the middle of her behind. He eyed the door and wished he were on the other side of it, but he couldn't refuse to help without explaining that his thoughts were far from friendly. He didn't want to embarrass her that way. This was his problem, and he would deal with it. His blood roared in his ears, and his legs felt numb as he moved forward on feet as heavy as concrete blocks.

She looked at him over her shoulder, and a lone curl glided over the pale skin between her shoulder blades. "I'm sorry. I should have changed before we left The Vines, but I had to get out of there. If anyone had asked us to kiss or mug for the camera one more time I think I would have screamed. I had no idea my family were such voyeurs."

"Mine, too." There had been an endless succession of guests—even in their small group—tapping on champagne glasses, demanding the required kiss and making the usual toasts. He'd been careful to plant those kisses on Mercedes's cheek. Her soft, fragrant cheek.

"It was nice of Lucas to provide us with sparkling cider. I doubt any of the guests noticed we weren't drinking real champagne."

"Yeah." His hands trembled as he reached for the top button. His fingers fumbled the first slippery devil free and then the next and the next, revealing inch after inch of bare skin. No bra, just as he suspected. His mouth dried. His throat closed. He tried to avoid touching Mercedes as he worked his way toward the buttons at her waist, but the snug fit of her dress destroyed his plan. Her warm and supple skin teased his knuckles. His pulse pounded in his groin, and his lungs burned from trying not to inhale her intoxicating perfume.

The dress gaped and the straps slipped off her shoulders. Mercedes caught the gown against her front before the fabric could fall to the floor, but not before a flash of deep red beneath the thin band of an ivory thong plunged Jared over the cliff of sanity.

The tattoo.

He swallowed a groan. He'd forgotten. Chloe had told him about the tattoo on Mercedes's right buttock, about the heartache and the pitcher of margaritas that had led Mercedes into getting a permanent reminder that love hurt. The tattoo was a red rose with thorns, Chloe said, and then Chloe had confessed she'd chickened out before getting her own tattoo. She'd asked if he thought she'd be sexier with a tattoo, and he'd assured his sweet, delicate wife that he'd never considered body art attractive.

The fierce desire to peel away the fabric of Mercedes's dress, to see and touch the rose on her skin belied those words.

"Thank you." Her husky voice made him grit his teeth.

Sucking in one painful breath and then another, he fisted his hands, then stepped away. *Chloe.* Think about your wife—*your first wife*—and how losing her almost destroyed you. You are weak, Maxwell. You might not survive loving and losing again. And Mercedes's relationships ended real fast when she found out her dates had feet of clay.

"I'll get your luggage," he ground out through clenched teeth and then spun on his heel and headed out into the night.

Don't do this to me, Mercedes railed at her misbehaving hormones. Something she would just as soon not name stirred low in her belly, a remnant of Jared's featherlight touch on her spine.

She'd never been the type to get hot and bothered by a look or a passing touch. Why now? And why Jared?

She'd never stayed friends with her past lovers. Her relationships ended bitterly—usually because the men let her down or her inability to commit became an issue. One thing was certain. Giving in to these outlandish new feelings for Jared guaranteed she'd lose her best friend.

And she couldn't lose Jared. He kept her sane. He was the only one she could let down her hair with except for her college friend, Dixie, but her brother Cole had married Dixie back in January, and Cole represented the family and the constant pressure Mercedes experienced to take Louret to the top.

Clutching the dress to her breasts, she retreated to her new bedroom and caught her breath. Jared had found the furnishings Chloe had originally bought for this room. Mercedes remembered her friend's enthusiasm in choosing each fabric, each knickknack. The cheerful colors and romantic ruffles were so reminiscent of Chloe that Mercedes's eyes stung.

Would Chloe see this marriage as a betrayal of their friendship? No. Chloe had valued family and children over almost everything else. She'd understand Mercedes's need to protect her unborn child.

Mercedes looked outside, but didn't spot the reporter Jared had mentioned, and then she closed the window blinds. A tap on the door made her jump. She clutched the bodice of her dress with both hands and turned. "Yes?"

Jared entered the room and laid her suitcases on the bed without making eye contact. "I'll start dinner before I change clothes."

The thought of putting food in her agitated stomach warred with the knowledge that if she didn't eat soon she'd be ill. If she had her druthers, she'd close the door, climb under the covers and hide from her tumultuous feelings. "Thank you. I'll be out in a minute."

Jared left, closing the door behind him.

Mercedes stepped out of her gown and hung it up. She mechanically dug through her cases until she found slacks, a blouse and a bra that still fit her swollen breasts. She didn't dress to impress. That wasn't her goal here. One by one, she pulled the pearl-tipped pins from her hair and dropped them on the vanity. She ran her fingers through her curls, trying in vain to make order out of chaos. Her hair was a rat's nest, as usual, but she couldn't remember if she'd packed her barrettes, and the noisy growls from her stomach warned her not to waste time searching. Not for the first time she wished she had Jillian's tame waves or Chloe's satin-slick hair. Instead she'd been cursed with hair that she couldn't run a brush through without turning it into a hedge. Natural curls were the pits.

The beeping timer on the microwave penetrated the bedroom door. She yanked the panel open, took one step forward and collided with Jared in the tiny dark hall between the bedrooms and the bathroom.

He grabbed her upper arms to steady her, but quickly released her and stepped back. "You okay?"

"Yes." Mercedes took in the way his snug white T-shirt delineated his muscular chest and shoulders and how his jeans snuggled his strong thighs and long legs. His feet were bare as were hers.

He'd been undressing while she'd been undressing. *Stop.* Irritated by her irrational thoughts, she shoved her unruly hair off her face.

He averted his gaze and jerked his head toward the kitchen. "Dinner's ready."

She resisted the urge to rub her hands over the warm spots where he'd touched her.

With a sweep of his arm, he indicated she precede him. Mercedes marched toward the compact kitchen. The simple addition of the rings on her finger made forbidden things no longer forbidden. Even though she had no intention of acting on her wayward thoughts, her rampant hormones seemed determined to run amok as much as possible.

"The ring set is beautiful. Thank you."

"You're welcome. Glad you like it," he replied stiffly.

The setting sun cast a dim glow across the colorful kitchen until Jared closed the curtains, filling the room with shadows and sealing them in an intimate cocoon. Although Chloe had never lived in the guest house, her presence permeated this room as much as it did the bedroom. The red and white plaid curtains matched the chintz chair cushions and the cheerful cherry wallpaper. Jared hadn't made many changes since he'd moved in after Chloe's death.

"Sit," he ordered.

Mercedes lifted a brow and sat at the table. "Are you always going to be in charge of the kitchen?"

He grimaced. "Sorry. Habit. Make yourself at home."

Forget you're married. Forget the man kissed better than any fantasy lover in your imagination. Pretend this is just another Wednesday-night dinner even though it's Saturday. Mercedes, trying to lighten the heavy mood, forced a smile to her lips. "I don't cook half as well as you."

Jared rewarded her efforts with a tight smile. He slid a loaded platter of the finger-foods her mother had served at the reception into the center of the small table, passed her a plate with fat cherries painted in the center and a chilled bottle of water. "I seem to remember you're a pretty good cook."

She'd brought him countless meals back in the dark days

immediately after the funeral when he wouldn't have eaten if she hadn't fed him. "You're better, but I'm willing to share kitchen duty."

Despite the fact that Jared fed her every Wednesday night, Mercedes didn't actually dislike cooking, but this cramped space wasn't big enough for the two of them to work simultaneously without a lot of body contact. With the weird way she'd been reacting to him lately, that wasn't a good idea— not if she wanted to get out of this marriage with her friendship intact.

"Would you like me to make up a schedule of who cooks when and post it on the refrigerator?"

"Mercedes," he practically growled, "rule number one. When you're here you relax. No uptight marketing and PR directors allowed. Stress isn't good for you or your baby."

She wrinkled her nose. "Does that work both ways? No overworked CEOs allowed? For someone who's his own boss, you put in a lot of hours."

"I'll shed my power suit at 5:00 p.m. if you will." The twitch of his lips as he settled in the chair across from her should have erased her anxiety, but her mind stayed stuck on the thought of shedding clothing.

What was wrong with her?

Their bare feet tangled beneath the table, and tension exploded with the suddenness of a popping champagne cork. She yanked her feet beneath her chair and crossed her ankles against the sudden surge of energy skipping up her shins. Ducking her head, she busied herself with her silverware, and then she stopped herself. Finger foods didn't require utensils.

Jared rose and picked up his plate and glass. "I'm going to read over the inn's prospectus while I eat."

He climbed the stairs to the loft, leaving Mercedes alone in the kitchen.

Her heart sank. This marriage had already taken a toll on their friendship. They couldn't even share a meal together. Was avoiding the publicity and a legal battle worth the price they'd pay?

Jared awoke with a burning need to escape. The house. Mercedes. The erotic dreams which had kept him up all night, in more ways than one.

He rolled out of bed cursing the hovering reporters who'd trapped him inside the cottage last night, tugged on his running clothes and headed out the door. He'd barely begun his prerun warmup when a reporter climbed from a sedan parked in the driveway.

"Leaving your bride so soon, Maxwell?"

Jared set his jaw, ignored the jerk and stretched his hamstrings.

"Mercedes awake yet? I'd like her statement on your hasty marriage."

Jared straightened. "Louret Winery will issue a press release."

"What do you think her boyfriend is going to say about your nuptials?"

Damn it. He didn't want to get dragged into this before he cleared his head. "Mercedes's relationship with Bradford is over."

"Does Bradford know that?"

Another car turned into the drive. A lanky, bearded guy climbed from the driver's seat. The camera hanging from his neck labeled him a reporter. The need to shelter Mercedes from an early-morning inquisition vied with Jared's urge to run.

"Do you want to explain the rushed-and-hushed ceremony?"

Jared clamped down on the *go to hell* that sprang to his lips and abandoned his warmup. Straightening, he forced his mouth into what he hoped looked more like a charming smile than a teeth-grinding scowl. "Gentlemen, we're on our honeymoon. Cut us some slack, would you? We will make no additional comments at this time. And you're on private property. Get lost."

Turning on his heel, Jared snatched up the Sunday paper and reentered the pressure cooker, which, until last night, had been his home, his sanctuary. He closed the door, locked it and leaned back against the wooden panel. He had to warn Mercedes about a potential ambush before he took his run. As soon as he did he was out of here.

A whisper of sound made him open his eyes.

Mercedes shuffled from the bathroom to the den. Her satiny red robe intensified the waxen pallor of her face and her colorless pinched lips. She pushed a trembling hand through her tumbled hair and continued toward the kitchen with single-minded determination.

The combination of her attire and her fragility hit him like a one-two punch to the gut. During their weekend trips they avoided intimate situations and kept the boundaries of their friendship firmly in place. Discussions were never held in nightclothes.

"Mercedes, are you okay?"

She turned her head and blinked as if surprised to see him. "Fine…or I will be as soon as I find the Cheerios."

"Cereal?"

"Yes."

Chloe had been delicate, but she'd rarely been sick during her pregnancies. Jared's protective instincts kicked up a notch. "I don't have any. Can I fix you some eggs?"

She grimaced, swallowed hard and pressed a hand to her stomach. "No…thanks."

"Toast?"

She hesitated. "That might work. Are the reporters still out there?"

"Yes."

"Ugh. I need to go to my apartment. I have to clean out the fridge and the kitchen cabinets and bring the food here, and then I need to finish packing my clothing and personal belongings. The movers are coming tomorrow morning to carry my furniture to The Vines for storage."

He shoved bread in the toaster and turned to find her gaze on him. The fabric of the satiny robe clung to the curves of her breasts with too much detail for his peace of mind, and her hair looked sexily rumpled. He savagely cut off the thought and attacked breakfast preparations.

She settled on a barstool at the counter and cautiously sipped from the glass of orange juice he poured for her. The overhead light reflected off the diamond engagement ring and matching gold wedding band he'd given her. She hadn't wanted anything fancy, and he'd intended to purchase a plain band, but the interlocking set reminded him of the face Mercedes showed the world. Buttoned up. Everything in its place. Understated, not flashy. But given the right setting and the freedom from her duties at the family winery, Mercedes sparkled with the same inner fire as the emerald-cut diamond.

She smothered a yawn. "Did you get to take your run?"

He jerked his thoughts back in line. She knew him well enough to know he ran five miles each morning. "No. There are two reporters waiting in the yard."

Sadness filled her eyes. "Jared, please don't let this marriage alter your routine any more than you have to."

He swallowed a laugh at the absurdity of her comment. She'd shot his routine to hell the day she'd informed him of her pregnancy. The wedding kiss had blown his mind, and he could only imagine what Mercedes had thought when he'd shoved his tongue in her mouth. My God, he'd lost control and crossed the line. Shame burned his ears. He couldn't explain why he'd betrayed her friendship and Chloe's memory, and no matter how hard he tried he could not subdue his resurrected libido. He raked a hand through his hair and fought the flicker of arousal licking through his blood that even shame couldn't quench.

But Mercedes had kissed him back, hadn't she? Or had her participation been purely to further this marriage charade in front of her family? She could hardly haul back and deck him without making them ask questions.

The toast popped up. He slid it onto a plate and shoved it across the breakfast bar. She mumbled her thanks and dipped her head to take a bite. A stray curl fell over her cheek.

He had to get out of the house before the need to smooth her tangled hair overwhelmed his good intentions. Five miles at a punishing pace ought to do the trick. "If the reporters don't leave, call the police and have them escorted off the property. After my run I'll drive you to your apartment."

"You don't have to do that."

"Your car won't carry your boxes. Should I rent a truck?"

"No, if we fold down the seats, your SUV should have enough room for the stuff I need to bring here…although I don't know where I'm going to put everything."

No kidding. The cottage was already cramped. They were practically on top of each other. Seeing her toothbrush in the holder next to his this morning had jolted any remnants of sleep fog from Jared's brain.

Mercedes licked a crumb from her plump bottom lip. The sight of her pink tongue hit him with breath-stealing force. He'd seen her do the same thing countless times before, but back then he hadn't known the taste and texture of Mercedes's mouth.

Someone knocked on the front door. Jared set down his glass of juice. "I'll get it. Finish your breakfast and have your shower. I'll take my run, shower and be ready to leave for your apartment in an hour."

He crossed the room and opened the door. A reporter shoved a tape recorder in his face. "Maxwell, did you marry Mercedes for her stake in Spencer Ashton's fortune?"

Anger roared in his ears. "No comment. Get off my property."

He slammed the door and turned in time to see Mercedes bolt for the bathroom. The sound of retching carried through the closed door and tied his stomach into knots. He hated feeling helpless. He didn't know what he could do except to get rid of the reporters and shield Mercedes from their intrusive presence and obnoxious questions.

After a quick call to local law enforcement, he rapped on the bathroom door. Mercedes eased it open. Her pale face put a lump in his throat. "Are you okay?"

She grimaced. "Sorry. My morning sickness—which you've noticed doesn't limit itself to mornings—seems to get worse when I'm stressed."

"Then I guess it's my job to keep your life as stress free as possible."

So much for his run and escape. He'd stick to Mercedes like a shadow today and keep the reporters at bay.

Five

M en! She was sick of the lot of them.

Mercedes slid into her desk chair on Monday afternoon with a relieved sigh. She'd never been so happy to return to work. Yesterday Jared had hovered during the packing of her things, getting too close and reminding her of his electrified touch on her skin and the heat of his mouth on hers.

He hadn't let her lift anything heavier than a wine bottle. And when the movers had arrived this morning, he'd informed them that she was allowed to point, but not to lift. Lucas had been equally overprotective when the truck pulled into The Vines to unload her belongings.

"They mean well," she grumbled, and tossed her purse and a bag of disgustingly healthy snacks into the bottom desk drawer. But Mercedes felt smothered, antsy and out of sorts. She was used to doing what she wanted and coming and going as she pleased with only her brothers' eagle eyes to dodge.

Having Jared, Lucas and the nosy reporters monitoring her every move set her on edge.

She smoothed a hand over her hair and tucked an escaped curl back into her French twist. Turning in her apartment key—and the freedom it represented—had been more difficult than she'd anticipated, but the loss of the home she'd loved only seemed to symbolize how out of control her life had become. Now she had nowhere to go to escape the strange awareness of her new husband except here in her office where she was *supposed* to be concentrating on work and not on the series of bumps and brushes against her husband that had kept her hormones simmering all morning. She flexed her fingers, causing her wedding rings to sparkle in the September sunlight, took a calming breath in an effort to ease her nausea and pulled a file forward.

The day couldn't possibly get worse.

Jillian breezed in. "Everything settled?"

I wish, Mercedes said silently but forced a smile for her sister. "As settled as it's going to get until Jared and I find a house."

Like their mother, her sister had taken a second chance on love and it had paid off. The bounce in Jillian's step and the flush on her cheeks attested to a happiness Mercedes and Jared would never have. They'd be lucky to get out of this with their friendship intact.

Jillian dropped a paper on Mercedes's desk. "Ashtons on page one again. Our half sis Megan is pregnant, too. I swear the papers would report our shoe sizes if they thought it would sell copies."

Mercedes's stomach pitched. She dug in her drawer for a pack of whole wheat—*blech*—crackers and a bottle of juice and then skimmed the article. How long could she keep her own pregnancy a secret before finding her condition splashed across the page in bold-face font? It was bad enough that her marriage to Jared had made the Sunday paper. Reporters had swarmed the two of them like fruit flies while they tried to empty her apartment, but the press had apparently accepted the friends-to-lovers story Jared had concocted.

She sipped, grimaced and cursed her finicky taste buds. None of her favorite foods appealed anymore. Even her orange juice tasted of burned plastic. "The movers had to wade through reporters to get into my apartment this morning. I've also seen a few loitering in the winery parking lot."

Jillian grimaced. "They're lurking around every corner. We've upped security, but with the increased activity due to the harvest, they can't be everywhere at once. Are you okay? You're pale."

Mercedes grimaced. "It's nothing a few months won't cure. Morning sickness is the pits, especially in the afternoon, but please, keep that to yourself. I'd rather not have Cole and Eli pulling the heavy big-brother act."

Jillian flashed a sympathetic smile. "Agreed. Let me know if I can help in any way."

"Thanks, Jillian. I promise to return the favor and keep Cole and Eli off your back when your turn comes." Her sister left with a dreamy smile on her face—no doubt dreaming of the day she and Seth had a baby to keep Rachel, Seth's daughter, company.

Mercedes propped her elbows on her desk and rested her head in her hands. She hadn't lied when she told Megan's sister, Paige, that she wanted to heal the breach in this family. That meant Mercedes needed to call Megan and congratulate her on her good news. But what could she say to a woman she'd known about for most of her life but hadn't met until earlier this year? Should she confess to being pregnant, as well? It would be wonderful to have someone to compare

notes with. Did her half sister suffer the same exhaustion, finicky taste buds and raging hormones?

She liked her younger half sister, Megan, and the two of
them seemed to have quite a bit in common besides a lousy father, but she hadn't told her own brothers about the pregnancy,
so it would probably be best to keep quiet a bit longer. She had
enough on her plate dealing with Jared and her new reactions
to him without stirring family and more reporters into the mix.

She dragged her Rolodex across her desk and flipped the
cards until she found Megan's work number. Pulling the
phone forward, Mercedes dialed.

"Megan Ash—um, Pearce," the voice on the other end
answered.

Mercedes smiled. Her half sister hadn't gotten used to her
married name yet. "Megan, it's Mercedes. I wanted to call and
offer my congratulations on your pregnancy."

A half groan, half chuckle traveled down the phone line.
"Those meddlesome reporters. They won't give Simon or me
a moment's peace. But thank you. We're thrilled."

Happiness filled Megan's voice, and a twinge of envy nibbled at Mercedes. Her baby would only have one parent ea-
gerly awaiting its arrival. But Craig wasn't good father
material, and this was the right choice. She squared her shoulders and laid a hand over her own stomach.

"Congratulations on your wedding," Megan added.

Warmth crept up Mercedes's cheeks. "Thank you."

"The picture of Jared carrying you over the threshold was
quite romantic."

Mercedes's skin prickled at the reminder of the picture that
had greeted her yesterday morning. From the photographer's
vantage point she and Jared had looked like a couple in love,
and for a moment as she'd stared at the picture she'd wished—
Mercedes cut off the thought.

She wished the spying reporters didn't make her nauseous. "Yes, it did look like something from a fairy tale."

She considered asking when Megan's baby was due, but bit back the question. If they managed to settle the family quarrel, then her child and Megan's could possibly be playmates, but she had plenty of time to worry about that later.

Mercedes twined the phone cord around her finger. "I'm hoping that once they find Spencer's murderer the press will leave us alone."

"We're hoping the same. It's difficult to live in a glass house, so to speak. And not knowing who killed our father or why is unsettling."

"Yes, it is. Megan, if you need anything…or if you just want to talk, please call me."

"Thank you, Mercedes. The offer goes both ways."

They said their goodbyes and Mercedes cradled the phone.

Three families had been torn to shreds by the selfish actions of one man. How could she have been so foolish as to let a man just like her father into her life? Not just one, but a series of them. As Jared said, her taste in men sucked.

Thank God for Jared. She didn't know what she'd do without him. And she didn't intend to find out.

Two cars occupied the winery parking lot—hers and another Mercedes recognized. Unfortunately.

Craig climbed from his expensive import. Mercedes silently groaned and cursed herself for working late as he crossed the lot. Tired, cranky and hungry, she stood her ground. "What do you want, Craig?"

He stopped a yard away. "Your marriage may have fooled the newshounds, but it didn't fool me."

Her stomach churned. "What is that supposed to mean?"

"That's my kid." He pointed to her midsection. "And you're

not keeping me from it. I'll get a DNA test. And then you'll have to pay palimony so I can keep the little Ashton heir in the manner to which he's accustomed during my visitation periods."

Her child was not an *it*. Anger stiffened Mercedes's spine, and bile rose in her throat. A part of her silently goaded, If you throw up on his expensive shoes he'll go away. But she didn't want to give him the power of knowing how much he upset her.

"Really? That's not what you said when you offered to pay for my abortion. As far as I'm concerned, Craig, the minute you uttered those words and shoved that check in my face you ceased to have anything to do with me or *my* baby."

"Tell it to the courts, sweetie."

"I will." The lie Jared had suggested resisted crossing her lips, but she forced herself to say the words. "Jared is going to be my child's father."

"We'll see about that, Mercedes. I devoted nine months of my life to you. That has to be worth something. And remember this, if you can't share, I'll sue for full custody. You'll hear from my lawyers."

Her blood ran cold. "And you'll hear from mine if you keep harassing me."

He turned on his heel, climbed into his car and peeled out of the parking lot.

Mercedes emptied her stomach behind a shrub. When the sickness relented she stumbled to her car and stabbed the key in the ignition with a trembling hand. She had to get home. And then it hit her. She didn't have a home anymore.

Damned hormones. She never cried, but she couldn't seem to stem the waterfall of tears.

Sissies cry. The childhood taunt from her brothers rang in her ears. Mercedes struggled to pull herself together. Self-pity solved nothing. She dug around her glove compartment until she found a paper napkin left over from some long-forgotten fast food lunch and mopped her face. She needed a plan—a foolproof plan—to keep Craig Bradford from using her baby as a pawn to get his hands on the Ashton money.

Jared's muscles clenched the minute he heard Mercedes's key in the front door. Dreading the quiet evening ahead, he rose from his desk, descended the stairs from the loft and jerked to a halt.

Red rimmed her eyes and the tip of her nose was pink. She'd been crying. His senses went on full alert. Chloe had cried over anything from birthday cards to chick flicks, but Mercedes didn't cry. His first thought was of the baby. His gaze briefly dropped to her belly and fear crept up his spine. "What happened?"

"Craig ambushed me when I left work."

Fear turned to anger. He swore and she flinched. "What did the bastard say? Did he lay a hand on you?"

"He didn't touch me and all he said was more of the same."

"Did you tell him the baby is mine?"

She glanced away, set her purse on the table behind the sofa and fidgeted with the clasp. "Not exactly."

He shoved a hand through his hair. "Mercedes."

Fisting her hands, she faced him. "I hate lying."

"For your baby's sake, could you get past that this time?"

"I'll try, but he—" Her voice broke. Tears filled her eyes and spilled onto her pale cheeks. "Jared, he says he's going to sue for full custody if I don't grant him access. But all he wants is the money. He admitted as much when he said I'd have to pay him palimony to keep the Ashton heir in the manner to which he'd be accustomed."

His protective instincts kicked in, full force. Jared pulled her into his arms, cupped his palm over her cheek and pressed her face to his shoulder. He rested his cheek on her hair and searched his mind for a way out of this mess. He cared more about Mercedes than anyone else, and he'd be damned if he'd let that selfish bastard hurt her.

"He won't win, Mercedes. I'll call my attorney first thing tomorrow. We'll do whatever we have to do to stop Bradford." Fresh tears scalded his knuckles. He drew back, tipped up her chin and swiped the tears from her cheeks with his fingers. He caught her gaze.

"I won't let him take your baby," he promised, and hoped like hell he could keep that pledge.

Her bottom lip trembled and her breath came in shuddery gasps. Jared pressed a thumb to her quivering lip as if stilling its motion could calm her. The warmth of her breath swept the back of his hand, and the mood in the room shifted in an instant. Desire slammed him. He became aware of the damp, soft flesh beneath the pad of his thumb and of the length and heat of Mercedes against him, of her breasts against his chest and her thighs interlocking with his.

He sucked in a sharp breath. Her redolence surrounded him. His heart stumbled and then his blood raced to pool where their hips touched. Gritting his teeth, he lowered his hands to her shoulders and searched for willpower.

Mercedes's eyes rounded and darkened from moss to jade. Surprise faded into awareness. The pink tip of her tongue swiped across her bottom lip and her nostrils flared. Her fingers tightened on his waist, curling into his skin instead of pushing him away.

God help him, he couldn't find the strength to release her. His muscles seemed locked in place and his brain shut down. His mouth watered and he swallowed hard.

"Mercedes." His intended warning sounded more like a hungry growl.

She tipped back her head and inhaled deeply. Her breasts nudged his chest, and he gritted his teeth against the rocket of fire screaming through his blood. Pulse-pounding seconds passed.

Move away, Maxwell. But the need to taste her overpowered his common sense. He lowered his head one agonizing inch at a time, giving her plenty of time to object, praying she'd have the good sense to stop him.

"Jared." Her whisper wasn't one of protest. And then she lifted her hand and cradled his jaw, scorching his skin with her touch.

He turned his head, pressed his lips to her palm and swirled his tongue over her skin. Her taste filled his mouth and his hunger expanded until he could barely draw air into his lungs. Her fingers threaded through the hair at his nape. A shudder racked him.

His mouth touched hers, lifted and settled again. Mercedes's lips parted in welcome, and he sank into her softness. Slick and hot, her tongue danced with his, tangling, retreating. He groaned.

Back off, Maxwell. Instead he angled his head and deepened the kiss. Common sense battled need. He dragged his hands down her spine, intent on pushing her away and ending this insanity, but the curve of her bottom fit his palms so perfectly that he hesitated. Mercedes moved against him and rational thought evaporated. He kneaded her buttocks and pulled her closer.

His groin throbbed. Desire ravaged his insides. Mercedes shifted, and the stiff peaks of her breasts raked his chest, forcing a hungry sound from his throat. Jared grazed his fingers upward over the curve of her waist and ribs until he reached the warm underside of Mercedes's breasts. He cupped her and stroked his thumbs over the beaded tips. She moaned into his mouth and the sexy sound filled him with an insatiable appetite.

Mercedes's nails scraped the sensitive skin of his nape, shooting a charge of electricity down his spine. Her legs shifted again. Her thigh brushed his groin, and her taut belly rubbed his erection. Fire coursed through his veins, consuming everything except the need to be skin to skin. She nipped his bottom lip. The love bite shocked and *inflamed* him. Chloe had never been an aggressive lover.

Chloe. He reared back and set Mercedes away. Fighting for control, he struggled to breathe. He'd not only betrayed Chloe, he'd betrayed Mercedes's friendship. He thrust his hands through his hair and put the sofa between them. His palms burned from the imprint of her flesh.

"I'm sorry. That won't happen again." He averted his gaze from her pointed nipples.

Looking as stunned and confused as he felt, Mercedes spread one hand over her chest and touched the other to her lips. "I—it's okay."

He'd expected her to curse him not forgive him. "Dammit, it's not okay. I can't love you, Mercedes. *I can't.*"

She lowered her hands and chewed her lip. "I know. But the kiss is my fault, too. My pregnancy has bent my hormones all out of whack. I'm more sensitive to just about everything. I'll ask the doctor about it at my next visit. There must be something I can do."

A muscle in his jaw jumped wildly. Mercedes wanted to take the blame for his loss of control, but the fault lay squarely on his shoulders. He'd crossed the line.

"For crying out loud, Mercedes, there's nothing wrong with you. It's me." He turned on his heel, snatched up his keys and headed for the door. "Dinner is waiting in the oven. I'm going out."

"Jared, you don't have to leave."

He hesitated with his hand on the knob, but didn't turn around. Guilt hadn't completely extinguished his hunger, and he couldn't guarantee what would happen if he stayed. "I need some space."

Without waiting for her answer, he yanked open the door. A flashbulb went off in his face, nearly blinding him. He slammed the door and swore.

"Reporters?" Mercedes groaned. "I didn't see any when I drove up."

He clenched his fists and wrestled his demons. "When the sun goes down the vampires come out to feed. Make sure the curtains are closed. I'll be in my office."

"Come and eat first. Please."

How could he refuse without sounding childish? He gritted his teeth and prayed for sanity. On leaden feet he headed for the kitchen, vowing to keep his libido under control and his hands to himself.

Mercedes's insides quivered, but she set her chin. She wouldn't let Jared know how difficult sharing a meal with him was for her right now.

Never had a man's kisses or caresses affected her so strongly. Could she blame her heightened response on pregnancy hormones or was it caused by something more? She chanced a peek at the tense line of Jared's jaw. Did her intense reaction to his touch have anything to do with the fact that she trusted him implicitly?

Jared would never intentionally hurt her. She couldn't say that about any man she'd ever dated—not that she and Jared had ever dated or even discussed taking their friendship to the next level. He was her safety net and she hoped she was his. Sex would only screw up their relationship—the way it had every intimate liaison in her past. She'd been badly burned by love twice during college, and she wasn't willing to buy into the third-time's-a-charm theory.

She followed him into the kitchen. Food held no appeal, but her baby needed nourishment. While he pulled plates from the cabinet and set the table, she opened the oven. Mouthwatering aromas filled the kitchen. Ever conscious of him moving around in the tiny space behind her, she set the casserole dishes on the stovetop and peeled back the foil.

Jared had cooked her favorite stuffed pork chops as well as a broccoli-and-cheese casserole. Her stomach rumbled in anticipation. Maybe her taste buds hadn't died after all. She opened the refrigerator, reached for a bottle of water and paused in surprise. Lime Jell-O. A smile tugged her lips. This morning she'd mentioned a weird craving for the jiggly green stuff. She lifted her gaze to his. "Thanks."

He shrugged. "As cravings go, yours seemed pretty tame. Chloe used to—"

He bit off the words and turned back to the silverware drawer. Love for Chloe had originally brought them together. Their shared grief and a promise Mercedes had made to her friend had bound them even after her death.

Mercedes didn't want him to feel uncomfortable talking about Chloe. "She used to have some pretty strange cravings. Remember when all she wanted to eat was crunchy peanut butter on strawberries?"

A smile lifted his lips, but sadness filled his eyes. "That wasn't as bad as sardines on chocolate ice cream."

They shared a grimace and some of the tension dissipated. Jared looked out for her as she did for him. She knew and accepted that he couldn't fall in love with her, and she didn't want him to, but he cared, the same way that she cared about him. He kept her from overstressing about work. She kept him from brooding too much about the family he'd lost. They kept each other on an even keel.

She dusted her hands. So no more of those unbalancing kisses. With a little nurturing, their friendship would carry them through this uncomfortable period the way it had through every other rough spot in their shared past.

But as Mercedes sat down across the kitchen table from Jared, she couldn't help wondering what it would be like to make love with a man who knew all her faults and liked her anyway. And once the pesky thought planted itself in her mind, it flourished like a weed and she couldn't seem to kill it.

She studied Jared's long-fingered hands in a way she never had before. How would they feel on her skin? What kind of lover would he be?

Don't go there, Mercedes. Jared's too important to mess this up.

She jerked her gaze away and it landed on the tiny swollen spot on his lip where she'd bitten him. Her cheeks warmed and her belly filled with shimmery warmth. Had he even had a lover since Chloe? From the way he'd eaten her up—her skin flushed anew just thinking about it—she didn't think so, and that being the case, she had no right to inflict her misbehaving, overly estrogenized self on him.

They were both running a little low on resistance right now, so she'd have to be strong enough for two.

Pretend the kisses never happened and forge on as before.

Friends. Just friends.

Yeah, right.

Avoidance. A simple plan.

Jared slowed to a walk and continued up the driveway.

Wiping the sweat from his face with the hem of his tank top, he congratulated himself on successfully dodging Mercedes again today. For the last three days he'd avoided her in the mornings by donning his running gear and taking off the minute he heard her stirring. For safety's sake he'd added an extra half hour to his run each day to allow her time to dress and get out of the house before he returned.

In the evenings he carried his dinner up to his loft office and tried to work, but he couldn't concentrate when he was vitally aware of her frustrated sighs, her restless energy and her every move in the den below. And he couldn't sleep worth a damn when he heard her pacing the floors at night.

He let himself into the cottage, grabbed a bottle of water from the fridge and headed toward the bathroom, stripping as he went. Peeling his tank over his head, he stepped into the bathroom, tossed the sweaty top into the hamper and turned to reach for the shower curtain. He jolted to a halt with his hand midair.

Mercedes's lingerie hung from the shower curtain rod. Peach, pink, cream and lavender bits of satin and lace caused a spike in his blood pressure. Chloe had worn white cotton underwear. Plain, white cotton. Nothing as lacy or sheer as the filmy sherbet-colored stuff in front of him. And Chloe definitely hadn't worn thongs like the one Mercedes had concealed beneath her wedding dress. The ivory bit of nothing now hung on the rod, drawing his eye like a flashing neon light.

Heat pumped through his veins and he swore. How was he supposed to take a shower with a week's worth of Mercedes's underwear guarding the cubicle like sentinels?

Worse, how was he supposed to look at her in the future and not wonder what tantalizing secrets she concealed beneath her clothing?

Cursing, Jared ripped the towels from a nearby towel bar

and tossed them onto the counter. One by one he transferred the silky pieces from the shower rod to the towel bar. He didn't linger over the task or allow himself to test the weight and feel of the garments between his fingers although the temptation to do so whipped through him hurricane strong. It wasn't until he'd relocated the last item that he realized his muscles had knotted from his jaw to his ankles.

He eased his jockstrap and shorts over his painful and traitorous erection, pitched them in the hamper and stepped into the shower. The frigid water made him gasp, but he welcomed the distracting sting and briskly lathered his chill-bumped skin.

How in the hell was he going to survive this marriage without crossing the line and making Mercedes hate him? He fell back on his tried-and-true method of overcoming difficulty.

Analyze the situation.

Divide it into manageable parts.

Set a course of action.

Problem one. Craig Bradford. Jared wanted to eliminate Bradford in the fastest manner possible. How, short of murder, could he accomplish the task? Research required.

Problem two. His marriage. The sooner he eradicated Bradford's threat the sooner he and Mercedes could separate, divorce and return to life as usual. Scrap that. The baby would irrevocably change Mercedes's life, and that meant Jared's had been permanently altered, as well. How could he minimize the damage?

Which led to problem three. The cottage. He'd call a real estate agent as soon as he dried off, and he cursed the fact that he hadn't done so already. Shortening their stay in this tiny, cramped cottage became more urgent and mandatory by the second.

Problem four. The press. With the media hounding them

at every turn, escape hatches had been sealed. How could they slip under the radar or shift the focus elsewhere?

His teeth chattered. He rinsed the shampoo from his hair. Now that his erection had subsided, Jared adjusted the water temperature and let the hot water thaw his chilled skin.

Step one. Call his attorney and see what legal steps they could take to block Bradford's claim on the baby. His attorney didn't handle custody issues, but someone in the firm would.

Step two. Call the real estate agent and find a house within a reasonable commuting distance for Mercedes to the winery. And room. Lots of room. Hell, he could afford it.

He turned off the spigot, scrubbed at the sting of soap in his eyes and reached for a towel. Out of habit he stretched toward the towel bar. Slick fabric in his hand had him jerking his eyes open despite the soap burn. A pink satin bra.

Swearing again, he shoved the garment back over the rack and snatched a towel from the counter. After drying off, he wrapped the towel around his hips and yanked open the bathroom door with almost enough force to rip it from its hinges. He stomped into the hall, accompanied by a cloud of steam.

Mercedes squealed and he jerked to a halt in the narrow hallway. Openmouthed, she gaped at him. "I...I forgot the notes I made last night."

Her gaze eased from his face to his shoulders over his belly, hips and legs. His body twitched to life. He gritted his teeth at his instantaneous reaction and thanked God he'd kept the towel around his hips. When he'd lived alone he rarely bothered, but with the threat of reporters shoving cameras against the windows, he didn't risk traipsing around in his birthday suit even though they'd kept all the blinds closed since their wedding day.

What color lingerie did she wear under her butter-yellow

suit? The thought flashed in his mind like a bolt of lightning—hot, searing and destructive. Dammit. He forced his gaze from the lacy cream-colored camisole covering her breasts to focus on her face.

A flush pinked her cheeks. She licked her bottom lip. When she looked at him like that—with a spark of curiosity in her eyes—he didn't feel like a bitter forty-year-old who'd lost interest in love and desire. He felt like a lusty college kid with his own healthy share of curiosity about the sparks between them. And if he continued to stand here, his towel wasn't going to be able to conceal his renewed interest.

"Excuse me." He tried to step around her.

She dodged in the same direction, grimaced and then, holding her hands up, backed out of the hall. The overhead light from the sitting room revealed dark shadows beneath her eyes and delayed his retreat.

"Mercedes, when did you have time to work last night?" They'd stayed up late to watch the news—a safe neutral activity.

She stared past his shoulder—no doubt noticing that he'd moved her underwear. A frown puckered her brow. "When I have trouble sleeping I work on the Louret marketing campaign. There has to be something I can do to divert the public's attention from our personal lives back to our products."

"You're not sleeping or eating enough, and you're still losing weight." His voice sounded harder than he intended, more accusatory than concerned, and the light of battle flared in her eyes.

Her lips flattened. "I can't help it. Nothing tastes good, and the morning sickness hits whenever it damn well pleases."

His stomach muscles tensed, and a bitter taste filled his mouth. "Are you having second thoughts about the pregnancy?"

Her eyes widened and she laid a protective hand over her

belly. "No. Oh, no. I want this baby, and I'm trying to do all the right things. I'm even drinking *milk*."

Her shudder startled a laugh out of him. "There are worse things than milk, Mercedes."

Her face was comical. "I'm sure, but you know I hate milk."

"Yeah, I know." He bunched the towel in his fingers and fought the urge to sweep a loose curl from her cheek. He had to keep a firm rein on the tender feelings she stirred in him.

If he touched her again...

He wouldn't. "I need to get dressed, and then I have a couple of calls to make. Afterward, I'll go to the grocery store and see if I can find something to tempt your taste buds."

"You don't have to do that, Jared."

"Yes, I do. For your sake. For your baby's sake." He'd do right by them, because there was a very good chance that one day soon—promise or no promise—he'd have to say goodbye to the best friend he'd ever had.

Six

Mercedes pulled her car into a space at the far end of the winery parking lot and said a prayer of thanks for the other vehicles occupying the remaining spaces. Business must be up today. Or had Jillian scheduled a group event this morning and Mercedes had forgotten it?

Lack of sleep and caffeine deprivation had killed her short-term memory. She smiled wryly in the rearview mirror as she checked her hair and makeup. Maybe she could blame her forgetfulness on pregnancy hormones, too, but she had a feeling the real cause was stress.

She gathered her purse and briefcase from the seat beside her. Work brought unrelenting pressure to try to find a way to divert the press from their private lives to their product. Life at the cottage wasn't much better. She spent every waking moment and many when she should have been sleeping working on a potential marketing campaign for the Meadowview

Inn just in case Jared bought it. It was a surprise. She hadn't told him yet.

The minute she relaxed, worries over Craig's threats forced themselves forward like a nagging toothache. Keeping her mind constantly occupied kept her from fretting over her father's murder, her impending motherhood and everything that could go wrong with her pregnancy and her life in general. She especially worried about her relationship with Jared. He was avoiding her. They'd missed their first Wednesday-night dinner in years this week. Oh, Jared had been home and in plain view, but he'd isolated himself in the loft claiming he had work to do, and she'd eaten alone. She missed their easy friendship.

The upshot was that her life had gone to hell. She barely allowed herself time to scratch or pee—which she seemed to need to do every thirty seconds these days—right now, in fact. She shoved open the car door and hurried toward the winery entrance.

With her mind on the long list of problems needing rectifying, she barely noticed a nearby car door opening as she passed. "Mercedes, are you pregnant?"

Her muscles locked at the stranger's question. She stood frozen on the sidewalk and stared at the young woman climbing from the vehicle.

"Whose baby is it? Bradford claims it's his," shouted another voice she didn't recognize from behind her. She turned. Alarm skipped up her spine. Cornered. Why hadn't she been paying attention? And where was the security officer? She searched what she could see of the vineyard grounds looking for the car with the flashing green light on top. No car.

"When is your baby due? Bradford says April. Can you confirm that?" A third reporter asked as he joined the others.

Craig had gone to the press. The bastard.

"No comment."

She hustled toward the safety of the building. The group of reporters surrounded her, hindering her escape. Mercedes did the only thing she could think of. She hit the panic button on her key ring and set off her deafening car alarm. Sirens screeched. The horn blew repeatedly. With the reporters momentarily distracted, Mercedes darted through them and ran for the winery entrance. Jillian, evidently drawn by the racket, opened the door. Mercedes shoved her keys in her sister's hands as she passed.

"Lock the door and call that security man." And then she bolted to the private bathroom upstairs and lost her lunch.

After she'd washed up, she dragged herself to her office and shut the door. She never shut her door, because she preferred knowing what was going on with Louret Vineyards at all times. She liked the hum of voices from down the hall and the occasional sounds drifting up from the tasting room downstairs.

So much for keeping her secret. She hadn't wanted her brothers to know she was pregnant yet. They were incredibly protective. If they suspected the baby was Craig's and that he'd abandoned her there was no telling what they'd do. Whatever their response, it promised to be newsworthy, which was the last thing the family needed right now.

She ignored the blinking message light on her phone, since it was probably reporters, and tried to gather her scattered thoughts. Twenty minutes later someone rapped on the wood.

"In my office," Cole's voice called out.

Mercedes winced and freshened her makeup, blatantly delaying the confrontation as long as possible. She arrived just in time to hear the rumble of Jared's deep voice through Cole's partially open door. *Jared was here?* He never came to the vineyard.

"The obstetrician tells me that high levels of stress could be dangerous for Mercedes and her baby."

Mercedes's mouth dropped open in horror.

"So Mercedes *is* pregnant?" Cole asked.

Mercedes shoved Cole's door open the rest of the way, glared at Jared and then faced her brothers, Cole, seated behind his desk, and Eli, seated beside Jared in front of the desk. The men rose as she entered. Jillian gave her a sympathetic smile.

"Yes, I am, and I would have told you when the time was right."

"Should I offer congratulations?" Cole asked.

Mercedes lifted her chin and looked him in the eye. "Of course."

"You realize the commotion in the parking lot means you need to hold a press conference?"

She grimaced. "I was hoping to avoid that."

Cole shook his head. "Too late."

Jared continued, "Mercedes isn't eating or sleeping well, and every time we get ambushed by reporters or Bradford she gets sick to her stomach—and Jillian says she did it again this afternoon. She's losing weight she doesn't have to spare, and if the situation continues, then according to her doctor she could have problems sustaining the pregnancy or, at the very least, it could cause the baby to be more sensitive to stress."

"What do you propose?" Eli asked.

They were discussing her as if she weren't here. Mercedes sputtered with anger.

Jared glanced at Eli and then his gaze tangled with Mercedes's. "I'd like to get her away from here for a few days so she can regain some strength and catch up on her sleep. The press is only going to get worse now that Bradford's telling tales."

Mercedes held on to her temper by a fraying thread, but she did note that Jared had chosen to stick to their story.

She focused on Eli. Usually she could get her oldest brother to side with her. Cole was a harder nut to crack. "Jared is wrong. I don't need time off work. I'm fine. It's only morning sickness, and it will pass."

"Now that he mentions it, I caught you dozing at your desk yesterday, and you have been looking pretty ragged lately," Eli added.

A frustrated sound gurgled from her throat. "Thanks, Eli. I love you, too."

He shrugged off her sarcasm. "I think it's a good idea for you and Jared to take a belated honeymoon. I don't think any of the rest of us would be stupid enough to refuse an excuse to get out of the spotlight."

Mercedes stiffened at the implied insult and fought the urge to stamp her foot. "I'm needed here."

"Not right now," Eli countered. "We're in the middle of the harvest. Take some time off."

"I have a job to do."

Cole shook his head. "The marketing campaign is moving along. Unless you can figure out who killed our father, then there's nothing you can do here to change the fishbowl in which we're currently living. Get out of town and take care of yourself and your baby."

"I have customers to visit, and I need to check in with our distributors."

"Eli or I can cover the customers and distributors. I hate to pull rank, sis, but if you insist, I'm going to ask for your keys."

"You can't do that." She shot a hard glance toward Jared. Did he have any idea what kind of trouble he'd stirred up?

Eli added, "Want me to call in the big guns—Mom and Lucas?"

This time Mercedes did stamp her foot and glare at Jared. He silently stared back. The concern in his eyes was the only thing that kept her from screaming in frustration. She'd lost her apartment, and now, thanks to Jared, she could lose her office, too. How could she hide from her crazy emotions if she had nowhere to go and no work to distract her?

But what was the point in arguing? Her brothers had sided against her, and if Eli called her mother and Lucas then she'd be out of a job indefinitely. Besides, catching up on sleep sounded like a good idea—even if being alone with Jared and her unwelcome fascination with him didn't appeal. Well, frankly, she corrected, it appealed too much and that was part of the problem.

"One week. That's it. I can't afford to be out of the office any longer."

Cole ignored her and looked at Jared. "Okay with you?"

Jared shrugged. "It's a start. I'll get back to you next weekend to let you know if she's made any progress."

Cole pinned her with his stern-big-brother look. "Then, Mercedes, starting now you are officially on vacation. But on your way out take a minute to make a statement to the press."

Mercedes trembled with a combination of fury at Jared for forcing her hand and fear over confronting the press. Normally facing the press wouldn't bother her, but normally it wasn't her private life under discussion. She either had to lie or risk saying something that would give Craig leverage over this child, and she didn't want to make that mistake.

"Could I speak to you in my office, please, Jared?" she said through her teeth, and then stormed from Cole's office and down the hall into her own. She quietly shut the door behind Jared when slamming it would have been *so* much more satisfying.

Bristling with anger, she confronted him. "What are you doing?"

He faced her stoically. "Trying to take care of you."

"Getting me kicked out of my office is not the way to go about it."

Irritation sparked in his eyes. "Then tell me what is, because you're putting yourself and your baby in jeopardy."

"I am managing just fine."

"If you call hugging the toilet several times a day fine."

"It's morning sickness, Jared. It's normal."

His jaw hardened. He didn't bother to point out that more often than not she was sick when it wasn't morning. "How much weight have you lost?"

Direct hit. Her clothes hung on her, except for across her swollen breasts, and, yes, she was concerned. She'd planned to call the doctor herself this afternoon. Mercedes shifted in her pumps. "I don't know."

Jared's gaze narrowed on her. "When I spoke to Dr. Evans this morning she said she'd hospitalize you if you continue losing weight."

He'd called her doctor. "Why do you care? You're trying to cut me out of your life, anyway. You won't even eat dinner with me anymore."

She detested the telling wobble in her voice.

Jared paced to her window, presenting her with the rigid line of his spine. He rubbed the nape of his neck. "I don't want to care, but I can't help myself."

Her heart contracted upon hearing him confirm her fears.

Slowly he turned. Mercedes caught her breath at the agony on his face. "You can't keep food down. You walk the floors at night. You jump at the slightest noise, as if you expect Bradford or the press to spring from behind the bushes. I haven't seen you eat a decent meal since breakfast at the Meadowview Inn two weeks ago." He moved closer and stopped just inches away. "I lost Chloe and Dylan, Mercedes.

Don't expect me to stand by and let something happen to you when I have the power to prevent it."

The fight drained out of her in a rush, leaving her tired and light-headed. Her eyes stung. Darn this new weepiness. She hated it.

When had hers and Jared's roles shifted? After Chloe's death Mercedes had become the caretaker in this relationship. At the moment her shift toward being dependent on Jared seemed like one more element of her life of which she'd lost control. She blinked back her tears and lifted her chin. "I'm trying to take care of myself."

Tension accentuated the lines bracketing his mouth. "Let me help. I have a lakeside cabin. Spend a few days there with me. We'll swim, kayak, hike…" He shrugged. "Whatever you want."

"I want to stay here and do my job."

His lips thinned. "Except that."

"What about your businesses? You can't turn your back on an entire string of bed and breakfast inns."

"I trust my innkeepers. You hired the best. If any emergencies crop up I can handle them by cell phone or laptop. You can do the same with your work. I'm not asking you to drop off the face of the planet, Mercedes, just temporarily step out of the line of fire and out of Bradford's sight."

She pressed her fingers to the dull throb in her temple. "What about the Meadowview purchase?"

"It's in my attorney's hands. I met with him this morning before coming here. I've also asked his partner to look into your legal right to keep Bradford out of the picture."

"Thank you for that."

"Get your things and let's go. We'll make a brief statement on the way out. Your suitcase is in the car."

She did a double take. "My what?"

"Jillian called me and explained the situation. I packed for both of us and came over. If we take the time to go back to the cottage the press will follow us. This way, they don't know we're leaving town. With luck we'll get out of the valley undetected."

She grimaced and conceded his point with a nod. How could she be angry with him when he had her best interests at heart? "I should really hate you for this, you know."

Jared's smile reached his eyes for the first time since she'd informed him of her pregnancy. God, was it only three weeks ago that her life had fallen apart? "But you don't."

"No. I don't think that's possible." Mercedes gathered her purse and shrugged on her jacket. With a sense of dread she followed Jared downstairs. How was she going to keep her insane hormones under control for the next seven days?

The number of reporters had grown in the past hour. More than a dozen converged around them the moment she and Jared stepped outside the door. Jillian, Cole and Eli stood behind Jared and Mercedes, silently offering family support and, unfortunately, blocking Mercedes's ability to retreat.

Mercedes caught herself sidling closer to Jared and cursed herself for her weakness. Before she could move away, Jared's strong arm banded around her waist. The heat of his fingers penetrated her clothing as he pressed her against the length of his body.

He brushed a kiss on her cheek and whispered in her ear, "Keep it simple and smile. You're supposed to be a blushing bride."

"Mercedes, are you pregnant?" the first reporter asked before Mercedes could make a statement.

She wet her lips and forced a smile. "Yes."

"Whose baby is it? Your husband's or your ex-lover's?"

Her stomach pitched.

"Mine," Jared said before she could formulate a reply. His free hand settled low over her belly, heating her skin and drawing her blood to the spot surrounding her navel. "Mercedes is my wife and this is our child."

"Bradford claims it's his."

"My name will be on the birth certificate."

"But genetically whose baby is it?"

Jared's muscles stiffened against her. "Mercedes and I have known each other for eleven years. We've traveled together and been—" he looked into her eyes and lifted a hand to twine a stray lock of her hair around his finger "—special friends for the past five years."

Mercedes's knees weakened at the tenderness in his eyes. *Oh, my.* Why had she never noticed Jared had bedroom eyes? And then she caught herself. The loverlike intensity was pure pretense. Good thing. How could a woman resist such a bone-melting look?

Jared smoothed his knuckle across her cheek and lowered his hand. His gaze returned to the press. "She's known Bradford for ten months and she dumped him. My guess is he regrets blowing it with the best woman he's ever known and now he's crying wolf."

With that parting salvo, Jared hustled her into his SUV and peeled out of the parking lot.

Jared's trepidation increased with each mile his SUV covered. He'd never shared the secret hideaway his grandfather had left him. Letting Mercedes into this private compartment of his life seemed like an omen.

Mercedes sat in the seat beside him. She hadn't spoken a word in almost two hours, but he could sense her tension easing as if the wind whipped it out through the open window as they headed northeast and left Napa Valley and the vineyard behind. The tight set of her jaw had relaxed, and her fingers had loosened on the edge of her purse. A breeze teased tendrils of hair from the tight twist on the back of her head. She'd quit trying to smooth it back in place about twenty miles ago.

She turned her head in his direction, and the dashboard lights illuminated her features. "Have you ever considered calling your father?"

Her question surprised him. He took his eyes off the road for a split second to shoot her a hard glance. "No."

"Not everyone is as coldhearted as Spencer. Or Craig. Your father might miss you."

His teeth clicked together. "If he does then he can pick up the phone."

"He won't if he's as stubborn as you."

He shifted in his seat, suddenly feeling his muscles cramp from the two-hour drive. "Mercedes, where is this coming from?"

"Something your brother Nate said at the wedding has been bothering me. He claims your father's lonely and that he misses you."

"He has Nate and Ethan and their families. My father cut me off, not the other way around."

"Jared, the only thing my father ever gave me was my name, and then he named me after his stupid car." Her sarcasm couldn't hide her pain. "Your father kept the three of you together after your mother died. When he traveled he took you with him. He didn't ship you off to boarding school or relegate your care to a nanny. For goodness' sake, he had your bus drop you off at his office everyday after school. He wanted you around. That has to mean something."

Mercedes's father hadn't wanted her around, and now Bradford only wanted their child for the money, connections and, evidently, the publicity he could get out of the relationship. Compassion for Mercedes welled up in Jared's chest, but he shoved it aside and focused on her incorrect assumption.

"It means my father wanted peons to carry out his commands, and he wanted his secretary to double as a babysitter. From the time my mother died when I was seven, my father ruled with an iron fist. Having us close by meant keeping us under his thumb."

She twisted in her seat until she faced him. "I'm guessing that as the unruly youngest son you felt your father's firm hand more often than your brothers. They seem like rule-followers to me. You've always liked the challenge of trying something new. But, Jared, I saw how much you enjoyed talking to Nate and Ethan after the wedding. I think you should try to mend fences with your father so they won't feel guilty for keeping in touch."

"I'll consider it." When hell freezes over.

"He's probably proud of you." Wistfulness tinged her voice, and Jared wished he'd had the foresight to tell Spencer Ashton what a jackass he was before he'd been murdered. "You've taken one struggling inn and turned it into a chain of bed and breakfasts. You're mirroring his success with the hotels."

"I built the chain with your help, Mercedes, and my father doesn't see my success. He sees my failure to toe the line."

"Maybe you're wrong about that."

He let the topic drop and checked his rearview mirror for headlights one last time, making certain the reporters hadn't followed. Mercedes was wrong, but Jared didn't want to waste time or energy arguing.

No matter how angry Mercedes might be with him for forcing this vacation on her, Jared was convinced he'd done the right thing in colluding with her brothers. After talking to Dr. Evans this morning, he'd known he didn't have a choice. Protecting Mercedes and her unborn child was worth whatever costs he had to pay. He wouldn't fail her the way he'd failed Chloe and Dylan.

He turned into the almost-hidden path through the towering pines. Darkness swallowed the vehicle. The moonlight barely penetrated the canopy of trees.

The headlights illuminated the small, rustic log cabin as he pulled to a stop at the end of the long driveway. Mercedes straightened and faced forward. "I didn't know you owned a cabin, and I thought I knew everything about you."

"Not everything. Let me unlock the doors and turn on the cabin lights, then I'll unload our supplies." He killed the engine, climbed from the vehicle and took a deep breath of the pine-scented forest air. It failed to have its usual calming effect, but that could have something to do with the woman standing beside him in the headlight beam.

Mercedes teetered on the path as her heels sank into the pine straw, forcing Jared to cup her elbow and guide her over the uneven ground. As had happened too frequently of late, she got too close, and her exotic scent filled his lungs and muddled his thinking.

She glanced around at the dense woods surrounding the cabin. "You're pretty isolated here, aren't you? I barely saw any lights once we left that little grocery store behind."

"Very isolated." They'd stopped at a small grocer's thirty miles back for supplies. Jared knew he could rely on the couple who owned the place to keep his whereabouts quiet. They'd known his grandfather for decades, and folks up here respected each other's privacy.

She squinted. "Is that the lake behind the cabin?"

"Yes." The cabin sat a hundred yards from the shore. The

rising moon painted a white, undulating stripe across the water. "It takes about two hours to kayak around the perimeter or three hours to hike it. I hike the trail every morning when I'm here."

He unlocked the cabin and reached inside to turn on the interior and exterior lights. Mercedes followed him into the single boxy room containing the kitchen and the den. Two smaller boxes, each containing a bedroom and bathroom, flanked the central space on the left and right.

"My bedroom's that way." He jerked his thumb to indicate the wing on the left. "This one's yours."

He stepped into her assigned space, hit the light switch and moved aside for her to enter. He scanned the area, trying to see what Mercedes saw. The small room had rough-hewn log walls. A double bed draped in a Native American blanket took up most of the floor space, and a tall dresser had been shoved in the corner. The wide window on the wall in front of him would offer a breathtaking view of the lake during the daylight hours, but now the curtains were drawn.

These Spartan accommodations bore no resemblance to his meticulously decorated cottage or Mercedes's monochromatic apartment. "Bath's through there. It's pretty basic."

He found her gaze on him instead of her new accommodations, and the intimacy of being in a ten-by-twelve room with Mercedes and a bed hit him like a two-by-four to the gut. No matter how wrong it was, he wanted her. There was no use denying it, but he didn't intend to feed that hunger.

"Chloe's never been here."

It was a statement, not a question, since it was clear from the sparse furnishings that Chloe hadn't contributed her decorating skills, but Jared responded anyway. "I inherited the place from my grandfather during the last half of Chloe's pregnancy. She didn't want to leave the inn."

And they both knew what came next. She'd died.

He came here when the memories weighed too much or when living in Chloe's perfectly decorated cottage grated on his raw nerves. The cabin held happy memories of childhood vacations with his brothers and his paternal grandfather, but no memories of the love and the life Jared had lost. He was careful to limit his trips to the days when Mercedes was on the road for Louret Vineyards. She was as protective of him as a momma bear was of her cubs. If she'd known he still had dark days—though far fewer than before—she'd have stuck to him like paint on wood. For the most part the cabin remained unused. He paid caretakers to keep an eye on the place.

He turned toward the door. "I'll unload the car."

"I'll help," she offered.

"No. Relax. Have a look around."

She looked ready to argue, but shrugged instead. He headed outside. Transferring the bags of groceries and their luggage to the cabin only took a couple of trips. When he finished he went looking for Mercedes. She'd draped her suit jacket over a chair in the den. The back door stood open, allowing a cool breeze to sweep through the screen door. Jared spotted the beam of a flashlight bobbing down by the lake and stepped outside. He paused on the rear deck long enough to light the gas grill and then joined her at the water's edge.

"It's beautiful," Mercedes said without looking at him. She'd let her hair down to drape over her bare shoulders and untucked her camisole from the waistband of her slim-fitting pants. A light evening breeze fluttered the hem of her top and made her disheveled curls dance in the moonlight.

"Yeah." He fisted his hands against the urge to twine one of those caramel-colored spirals around his finger. Why did sharing this quiet night with Mercedes feel so right?

Chloe had adored people. This place would have bored her

to tears, which is why he'd never brought her here when his grandfather was alive, but Mercedes had always appreciated the silence of out-of-the-way places. Guilt stabbed him. He shouldn't compare Chloe with Mercedes. The two women were opposites in too many ways to list. Chloe had needed to be needed. She'd relished pampering him and giving him the nurturing he'd lacked after his mother had died.

Mercedes treated him as an equal. She carried her own backpack—no matter how heavy—and expected him to do the same except for those times when he'd been too weak to shoulder his burdens. Then she'd stepped forward, dragged him back to his feet and gently administered a kick to the seat of his pants to get him going again. Mercedes didn't tolerate weakness in herself or those around her.

He picked up a pebble and skipped it over the water, sending ripples over the lake's mirrorlike surface. "Hungry? I've fired up the grill."

She looked at him, hesitated and then smiled. "Yes, I am, actually."

The surprise in her voice confirmed his decision to get her out of Napa. "I'll put on the steaks."

"I'll be right behind you."

"Take your time. We have all night." His mind spun the words into an entirely different meaning. Jared clamped his jaws shut and marched toward the cabin.

What would it be like to have the love of a man like Jared?

The errant thought exploded out of nowhere. Mercedes snuffed it and reached for her iced tea. She wasn't interested in falling in love with Jared. She loved and trusted him more than anyone, which meant having that trust broken—as inevitably would happen—would be all that much more devastating. She'd learned the hard way that, with few exceptions, men let her down. She couldn't bear to be disappointed by Jared too.

There was no denying that he cared for her. That much was obvious by the way he faced his fears over this pregnancy for her and her baby's sake. But he wasn't *in love*. And neither was she. Love was for tenderhearted souls like Jillian and Chloe, not for a realist like her.

She sat back and put a hand to her full stomach. The grilled steak had pleased her finicky taste buds, and she marveled at the amount of food she'd put away. "You're spoiling me."

His level gaze met hers. "You don't let anyone spoil you."

"You make that sound like a bad thing."

"A man likes to feel needed, Mercedes. You don't let anyone close—not even your lovers."

"And you do?" she quipped, but his reply hit too close to home. She didn't let anyone get close for a darned good reason. If she didn't love them, then saying goodbye wouldn't hurt. And saying goodbye was unavoidable.

"I don't let anyone close anymore," Jared said after a hesitation. "I need to turn off the grill. I'll be right back." He rose and stepped out the back door.

Mercedes dropped her head in her hands. She wasn't totally heartless, was she? She loved her family and Jared. But she'd never been *in love* in the unreserved, no-holds-barred way Jared had loved Chloe. She'd thought she was, in college, but she'd turned out to be wrong. Since then she dumped a guy whenever her feelings for him started to grow, because she was afraid to risk caring too much.

She wasn't a coward. She faced facts. Look at Jared. He still hurt from losing Chloe, and there had been times immediately after Chloe's and Dylan's deaths that the depth of his depression had worried Mercedes, times when she'd been afraid she'd never break through his pain.

Jared returned and dropped a deck of playing cards on the table. "Mercedes?"

Jared had come a long way since those dark days when he'd isolated himself from everyone—including her. He now kept himself in peak condition. Shallow crow's feet radiated from his thickly lashed blue eyes—eyes that still held shadows of sadness. A lock of dark hair tumbled over his forehead, and silver strands glistened at his temples. Lines bracketed his mouth, cutting into his lean, tanned face. Why had she never noticed what an incredibly attractive, mature man he'd become?

She shook herself out of a stupor. "Does a day ever go by that you don't think of her?"

He sucked in a sharp breath and then turned to the sink, busying himself with their dishes. He didn't ask to whom she referred. Finally he braced himself on the edge of the counter, clutching the countertop with a white-knuckled grip. "Yes, and it shouldn't."

"What do you mean?"

His head turned and his pain-filled gaze met hers. "It's my fault she and Dylan are gone. It doesn't seem right for me to keep living and to forget. Sometimes I'll think of her and realize that a week or even two has passed since I thought of her."

Mercedes blinked in confusion and crossed the room to stand beside him. "Why is Chloe's death your fault?"

"Because she asked me to go get a damned quilt and I refused."

Mercedes turned cold. Goose bumps raced across her skin. Her chest constricted and she thought she might pass out. She clutched the back of a kitchen chair for support. "She was going after a quilt when she had the car accident?"

"Yes. And before she left we fought about her buying more baby stuff, because money was tight back then. She wanted to borrow from my father and I didn't. Borrowing meant strings, and I…" He shoved a hand through his hair and shook his head. "She stormed out of the house to go to the store, anyway.

"I never got to apologize. By the time I reached the hospital she'd been declared brain dead. The doctors did an emergency cesarean to try to save Dylan, but he'd sustained too severe a head trauma to survive. He never got to take his first breath."

He threw back his head and tightly closed his eyes. Pain and tension stretched every muscle in his body taut. "My wife and son died over a damned quilt."

Guilt settled over Mercedes like a smothering blanket. The delicious dinner weighed like a boulder in her belly. Tears stung her eyes, and the lump in her throat burned as if she'd swallowed a hot charcoal.

As horrible as the truth was, Jared needed to hear it—even if it made him despise her. "You shouldn't hate yourself, Jared. You should hate me. I called Chloe from my cell phone that morning to tell her about the quilt in the consignment store window. I passed the shop on one of my vendor visits, but I was running late, and I didn't want to take the time to stop at the shop and buy the quilt. So, it's not your fault, Jared. It's mine."

The grief in his eyes deepened and then turned to empathy. He cupped her shoulder and squeezed. "It's not your fault, Mercedes."

"Then whose is it? Not yours." She shrugged off his touch and, hugging herself, walked to the screen door to stare out at the darkness. An owl hooted in a nearby tree. She'd never heard such a sad, lonely sound as the owl calling to his mate and receiving no reply. Because of her, Jared's calls for Chloe would go unanswered.

She pressed icy hands to her cheeks. "I can't believe I never knew."

"I never told anyone. It was my cross to bear." His voice drew nearer as he joined her by the door.

She blinked hard and ducked her head to hide her tears when what she really wanted to do was bury herself in Jared's strong arms and bawl like a baby. "And now it's mine."

Seven

Chloe, her dearest friend since third grade, was gone and it was Mercedes's fault.

Chloe's parents had lost their only daughter. Jared had lost his wife and son. Loss welled up inside Mercedes as if it were only yesterday that Jared had called her to tell her that Chloe and their baby boy had died.

Jared's long-fingered hands cupped Mercedes's shoulders. Numbly she allowed him to turn her and pull her into his arms. He caught her cheek in his palm and pressed her face against his chest. A sob worked its way up her throat.

"Shhh." His breath stirred her hair and his heart beat steadily beneath her ear.

"I'm so sorry," she choked out against the front of his shirt. "I took away the two most important people in your life."

His big hand stroked up and down her spine, but Mercedes

felt cold deep in her soul—too chilled to be warmed by his brisk caress. "Mercedes, I'm not letting you take the blame for this. Chloe wasn't your responsibility. She was mine."

"I told her the design was perfect...the exact colors she wanted for Dylan's nursery." Chloe had always done everything she could to make those she loved happy. In return for that generosity, Mercedes had selfishly put her needs and her driving desire to prove herself to her brothers *and her father* in front of anything or anyone else—even her dearest friend from childhood.

If she could relive those moments today, she would gladly give back the ten minutes it would have taken her to stop and buy the baby quilt, if it meant having Chloe and Dylan here. But it was too late.

She swallowed the sob climbing her throat and lifted her chin to look into Jared's sad blue eyes.

His touch gentled, slowed. The grief in his eyes faded, and desire took its place. His nostrils flared as he inhaled deeply. The fine hairs on Mercedes's skin rose, and her breath hitched. The warmth and scent of him surrounded her. She suddenly became aware of the press of his muscular body against hers and the strength of the arms enfolding her. Her body awoke, clamoring with forbidden hunger. A flush radiated from her core.

Damned pregnancy hormones.

She couldn't seem to control the need blossoming inside her, but the length of Jared's hardening flesh against her navel indicated he fought the same battle. She'd caused him untold heartache, which she couldn't cure, but she could offer him comfort in the only way she knew how.

Friends who became lovers, he'd said, and suddenly the idea didn't sound as crazy as it had before.

Doubt nipped at the edges of her consciousness, and her

heart beat with hummingbird swiftness as she slowly rose on tiptoe, cupped his jaw in her palms and pressed her lips to his.

"I'm sorry," she chanted between kisses, "so sorry."

"Mercedes," Jared tried to protest, but his voice was little more than a croak. Another kiss from Mercedes's soft lips and another whispered apology smothered his words. Her tears dampened his lips and tasted salty on Jared's tongue.

Determined to end this insanity before he lost his tenuous grip on control, he caught her upper arms, but he couldn't muster the strength to push her away. Her breasts brushed his chest and her thighs tangled with his. Silky, tumbled curls teased the backs of his hands and his wrists, sending a frisson of need over him.

He cursed his base response to Mercedes's offer of solace. She'd despise him if she knew how badly he wanted to tangle his fingers in her soft hair and lose himself in her mouth and inside her body. It was a betrayal, dammit, a betrayal of his wife and of Mercedes.

"Mercedes," he said, firmly holding her an inch away. Their gazes met and held. The desire flickering in the depths of her deep-green eyes caused his pulse to pound like automatic gunfire. "We have to stop."

"I'm not Chloe. I can never be Chloe, but let me ease your pain."

He couldn't draw a breath and his knees nearly folded. He'd read about the need to reaffirm life by making love, but he'd never experienced it. He'd bet his newest B&B that was what Mercedes wrestled with now. "You don't know what you're saying."

She traced his ear, his jaw and then the curve of his bottom lip with her finger. "I do."

His heart beat faster and an explosive pressure built in his gut. *Just say no.*

"Make love with me, Jared."

Damnation. He grasped for reason. "The baby..."

"You heard what Dr. Evans said. We won't hurt the baby."

He needed to be strong now more than ever before, but when Mercedes leaned against him and sipped from his lips again, his resistance wavered. The hard tips of her breasts gouged twin paths of fire across his skin, and he could barely breathe. He struggled to analyze the situation, divide it into manageable parts or set a course of action.

Analyze... He and Mercedes were about to make an irrevocable mistake.

Blood pooled in his groin, and his pulse roared in his ears. His conscience urged him to run, but the need percolating under his skin kept him right where he stood. He shook his head, trying to break the crazy magnetic pull between them, but he failed. Miserably.

Divide...

Mercedes. Vibrant. Alive. Sexy as sin. She didn't love him, but then she never loved any of her lovers. Could their friendship survive intimacy? A moot point. Jared feared their relationship, like their marriage, was already running on borrowed time.

She licked a hot, damp trail across his bottom lip, and her tongue tangled with his. One kiss wouldn't hurt. His hands slipped from her shoulders and into her hair. Her curls twined around his fingers, holding him captive. He opened his mouth over hers and deepened the kiss, drinking in the taste of her like a starving man.

Instead of recoiling from his unleashed passion, Mercedes molded herself against him, fusing her body to his and winding her arms around his neck. She matched him kiss for hungry kiss. Her nails teased his nape, and a shudder racked him. His heart pumped harder, and his skin felt electrified, but his muscles weakened. No woman had ever affected him this way. Not Chloe or any of the lovers he'd had before he'd met her.

Set a course...

They were moving too fast and bound to have regrets if they didn't stop *now*. He gasped for air, clasped Mercedes's hips and struggled to clear his head by putting a little distance between them. His thumbs landed on the bare skin between her pants and top. Against his better judgment he stroked satiny warm flesh beneath her rib cage until she shivered. He wanted to caress her skin and inhale the exotic, spicy essence of Mercedes. He shouldn't, but she had him so rattled that the reasons why he should deny his desire and hers ebbed out of his grasp.

Mercedes reached for the hem of her camisole, pulled the fabric over her head and dropped the lacy top to the floor. Her sheer, butter-yellow bra hid nothing. He could clearly see the dusky pink areolas surrounding her tightly contracted nipples. Her breasts rose and fell rapidly as she panted for breath. He gritted his teeth on a groan and wrestled his rabid craving. Sweat dampened his brow and upper lip.

She grabbed fistfuls of his shirt and yanked the hem free of his pants. The light scrape of her nails on his flesh hit him like live electric wires. She whisked the fabric over his head and then tossed it on the floor beside her discarded top. Her fingers spread across his chest, tunneling through his chest hair with brain-melting amperage. She reached between them, unhooked the front closure of her bra and shrugged it off.

His hands ached to hold her round, firm breasts, but there was a reason why he shouldn't. He just couldn't remember what it was. She leaned forward to press a kiss over his nipple. The contact with her lips and body seared his skin. His breath whistled through clenched teeth. She danced her fingers over his waist, stroking him with a featherlight touch and stoking the urgency of his hunger. He folded like a house of cards, and his remaining reservations evaporated.

Jared backed toward the sofa, dragging Mercedes with him. He skimmed his fingers from her hair down her spine to the indentation of her narrow waist. Her supple skin rippled beneath his touch. He caught her moan with his mouth and devoured her. Slow, sensual kisses evolved into rough, impatient bites. He delved a finger beneath the waistband of her slacks, sliding it back and forth beneath the fabric. She drew back to tackle the button and fly of his pants. His stomach muscles contracted involuntarily as did hers when he returned the favor.

A blasphemy slipped past his lips as he fumbled like a clumsy adolescent, and then her pants and his lay discarded on the floor beside their shoes. The minuscule yellow panties barely containing her light brown curls nearly undid him. He yanked her close, sucked a sharp breath at the hot fusion of their torsos and took her mouth in another greedy kiss. He cupped her buttocks—*her bare buttocks*—and a groan erupted from his chest. Another thong.

He traced the strip of fabric dividing her cheeks and she whimpered. The tattoo. He wanted to see her tattoo. He'd dreamed about the damned thing every night since the wedding. But Mercedes's fingers tunneled beneath the waistband of his boxers and curled around him. The glide of her fingers down his rigid shaft cut off rational thought. Every muscle in his body tensed rock hard, and raging need consumed him. He grasped her wrist.

"Too much," he ground out.

She released him, but only to shove his shorts to the floor. He kicked them aside, hooked his fingers beneath the thin strips of her thong and whisked the fabric down her legs. She stepped free. Jared sat on the sofa, cupped her bottom and pulled her between his splayed legs. Beautiful. Pale, creamy skin. Her curves were slight but sexy as hell, and her tummy was still too flat to reveal the secret within.

He hesitated again, thinking of the baby, but Mercedes tangled her fingers in his hair and offered him her breast—an irresistible invitation. He teased her, laving and nipping before finally sucking her deep into his mouth. A sexy sound gurgled from her throat. More arousing noises slipped from her lips when he transferred his attention to the other breast.

Ravenous hunger chewed at his insides. Impatience urged him to hurry. He deliberately did the opposite, forcing himself to bank the fires, to savor the taste and texture of Mercedes skin and the slick moisture he found between her legs. She arched into his searching fingers, threw back her head and whispered, "Yes, right there. Just like that."

She rained down encouraging words, inciting his hunger to fever pitch. Sexy whispers were a new experience for him, and if he didn't get the show on the road he was going to go off early and solo—like a first-timer.

He trailed a string of kisses past her navel, buried his nose in her curls and inhaled her essence. Spicy. Exotic. Uniquely Mercedes. He lifted one of her legs and propped her foot on the cushion beside him. The position left her open for him to explore with his mouth and his hands. Her knees buckled at the first swipe of his tongue and only his firm grip on her buttocks kept her upright. She dug her fingers into his shoulders and let her head fall back. Her muscles quivered with each caress, and moments later, release rippled through her, flooding him with the taste of her pleasure.

"Jared, please." Her luminous, passion-filled gaze locked with his. She cupped his shoulders, urging him back against the cushions, and then she straddled his lap and lowered herself over his throbbing shaft.

A slick inferno engulfed him inch by excruciating inch. Her slow descent nearly drove him out of his mind. The necessity to pound mercilessly into her consumed him. Mercedes must have read his mind and perversely decided to torture him instead. She rose and lowered, taking him infinitesimally deeper each time until she possessed him completely. He was ready to plead for mercy by the time she slowly picked up speed.

He captured her hips in his hands and her nipple in his mouth. The sexy sounds she made and the aroma of their passion pushed him to the edge. He was close, so damned close to blowing a circuit, but he wasn't doing this alone.

He combed his fingers through her damp curls, found the center of her passion and urged her to join him in his madness. She stiffened and then her orgasm rippled through her, sparking the explosion of his climax. Lightning flashed behind his eyelids and filled his veins with incinerating heat. He arched off the sofa, gripped her hips and pulled down on her narrow waist, burying himself to the hilt.

Mercedes collapsed against his chest with her head on his shoulder. Their panting chests rose and fell in unison and their damp skin melded. He buried his nose in her hair, hoping her distinctive perfume would tease him back to consciousness, but the mission was doomed. His lids grew heavy. His muscles turned to lead. He closed his eyes and allowed himself a few minutes to take pleasure in holding a woman close again.

Mercedes…his friend and now his lover. A mistake… Or a miracle? Probably the former. His brain fogged and time passed, but whether it was six minutes or sixty, he couldn't say. When he roused, Mercedes slept in a boneless heap in his lap. Warm, soft, sated. He hated to disturb her, but neither of them had been sleeping much lately. They needed their beds. He slid to the edge of the sofa and stood, lifting her and hitching her legs over his hips. She stirred, tightening her arms around his neck and her legs around his waist. "Where are we going?"

"Bed. Shhh," he said against her cheek and carried her to her room. Jared yanked back the covers and lowered her onto the sheets. His body separated from hers, and instantly he missed the intimate embrace.

She caught his hand when he tried to rise. "Stay with me. Please."

He hesitated. Without a doubt he'd just made the second biggest mistake of his life. The first had been letting Chloe storm out of the house after their argument over the quilt. But Mercedes now believed herself responsible for Chloe's death. No one knew better than he what a torturously destructive burden that guilt could be. Hell, he'd walked to the edge of a cliff over it, and he didn't want Mercedes doing the same. He had to convince her that he was the one responsible for the accident that had taken her childhood friend.

Against his better judgment, Jared slid into bed beside her. She wiggled closer until her warm, lithe body filled his arms and a silky leg hooked over his. The rake of her fingers over his hip revived his sluggish brain, and suddenly sleep was the last thing on his mind. He glanced at Mercedes's face. The sultry tilt to her lips told him that sleep wasn't high on her agenda, either. His heart and a particularly demanding part of his anatomy jerked.

Tomorrow. He'd convince Mercedes that Chloe's death was his fault tomorrow.

Tonight he wanted to feel alive one more time.

* * *

Mercedes awoke to silence and cold sheets. Where was Jared?

She sat up in bed and winced as her muscles protested their passionate night. Making love with a man she trusted had been so…freeing, so…comfortable. *So incredibly different.* Never in her entire life had she been so uninhibited in bed. Her only concern had been bringing Jared pleasure. In return, he'd multiplied her fulfillment tenfold. She shoved back her tangled hair.

She and Chloe had never shared the intimate details of their love lives, so Mercedes hadn't known Jared would be a generous and adventurous lover. He'd found erogenous zones she hadn't known she possessed, and she knew her body pretty well. And when he'd traced her tattoo with his tongue… A delicious shiver skipped down her spine at the erotically charged memory. She'd never had a lover do that before and had no clue how potent the caress could be. A blush warmed her from head to toe.

Good grief, she never blushed.

Together she and Jared had been white-hot. Stupendous. Orgasmic. She ducked her chin and smiled. Another wave of warmth swept her skin and settled in the pit of her stomach, but then the sexual hum morphed into an anxious knot.

They'd shared nothing more than comfort and great sex last night, right? But if it was nothing more, then why had making love with Jared far exceeded anything in her experience? She chalked up her outrageous response to pregnancy hormones.

Last night's intimacy would not change their friendship. She wouldn't let it. Jared was her escape valve. His B&B buying trips and their Wednesday-night dinners took her off the tense, competitive playing field where she butted heads with her brothers. Jared was an integral part of her life.

She swung her legs to the floor, stretched out the kinks and then crossed the room to dig in her suitcase for something to wear. She found her red robe and shrugged it on. Her hand paused over a collection of lingerie. Jared had packed these. How did she feel about him going through her underwear drawer? She considered it, but then shrugged it off. He'd packed her suitcase. No big deal. She'd do the same for him if the need arose. Friends did that kind of thing for each other.

Would Jared regret last night? Probably. He'd tried to talk to her as their pulses slowed and their bodies cooled, but she'd been afraid of what he might say, so she'd interrupted him each time with more hot kisses until they'd finally collapsed in exhaustion sometime in the middle of the night.

Massaging the crampiness below her navel, Mercedes went looking for him. She had to make sure he understood she didn't expect more than he was willing to give. They shared so many common interests. Biking, hiking, rafting, climbing—all physical activities. Sex could be just one more hobby they pursued together. Couldn't it? Although she'd never considered sex like climbing a mountain—something you did just because you could.

She hesitated in her bedroom doorway, chewing her lip. Maybe they should forget last night ever happened. No, last night had been too amazing to forget. As long as she remembered Jared would always love Chloe, and he remembered she wasn't going to risk loving anyone, they should be okay. No one would fall in love and no one would get hurt.

The kitchen and den were empty, as were Jared's bed and bathroom. His bed hadn't been slept in, so he must have stayed with her after she fell asleep. Comforted by the knowledge, she stepped out onto the back deck and scanned the yard and what she could see of the waterfront. No Jared. Where could he have gone?

Backtracking, she located his car in the driveway. Without

transportation he couldn't have gone far. If he hadn't returned by the time she showered and ate breakfast she'd go looking for him. She worried about him when he brooded, and she'd worry even more now that she knew he blamed himself for Chloe's death. That certainly explained why he'd closed himself off after the funeral. And of course their lovemaking could have heaped on more guilt. He probably thought he'd betrayed Chloe.

An itchy feeling settled over Mercedes's shoulders. Had she betrayed Chloe's friendship? She tugged her robe tighter against a sudden chill, and then opened the box of Cheerios and munched on a handful to settle her stomach. Not once during Chloe's life had Mercedes ever made an inappropriate move or had an inappropriate thought toward Jared—unlike the way Craig had hit on Mercedes's friends. And more than once Chloe had asked Mercedes to look after Jared if something happened to her. So, no, Mercedes decided she hadn't betrayed her friend. She was fulfilling a promise. Wasn't she?

She headed for a hot shower to ease her achy muscles. Ten minutes later she'd washed and dressed in shorts, a long-sleeved T-shirt and hiking boots. She slathered on sunscreen and still Jared hadn't returned. Mercedes swung through the kitchen for a bottle of water and saw his note on the refrigerator. How had she missed that before?

Hiking.

He'd said he hiked the perimeter of the lake each time he came up here. Jared was left-handed. When they hiked together he invariably chose the left fork in a trail unless they had a specific destination in mind—just like he'd chosen the left bedroom in the cabin. Smiling because she knew his habits so well, Mercedes let herself out of the cabin and set off to the right, hoping to intersect him.

The tightness in her abdominal muscles didn't loosen as

she hiked the clear but meandering path through the tall trees. In fact, it worsened. Even though she'd never had anything like that happen before, she blamed the discomfort on last night and brushed her concerns aside. She was in excellent health and great physical condition. A hike with no incline to speak of certainly wasn't beyond her abilities. The doctor had said so.

She hugged her arms around her chest as the pine-scented air grew cooler in the shade and trudged on. How much of a head start did Jared have?

The ache below her navel increased. They had overdone it last night. She needed to pee, but that was no surprise since the urge hit her ever thirty minutes or so. But she didn't relish the thought of ducking deeper into the woods. Thus far, she hadn't encountered any other hikers, but it'd be her luck to startle a pack of Boy Scouts by dropping her pants.

Her watch indicated that she'd been on the trail for less than an hour. Unless Jared had taken the right fork, she should meet up with him soon. The cramping in her belly increased, making her more than a little nervous and sending a trickle of fear down her spine.

It's nothing. Keep walking. But she didn't. Her steps slowed and Mercedes sank down on a sunlit boulder. She'd take a five-minute rest and then resume her hike. If the break alleviated her pain, then she didn't have to worry about her baby. If it didn't… She was very likely going to panic. In a worst-case scenario, she could use the cell phone in her pocket to call for help. Never mind she didn't know where she was or that she might have trouble with reception here in the valley. She'd worry about that if it became necessary.

Her discomfort lessened as she sat and contemplated the steep tree-covered slopes surrounding the lake. What was she going to say to Jared when she found him? Should they try to make this marriage work? It would involve carefully drawing boundaries and respecting them. Her child would certainly benefit by having a stable father. And she didn't doubt for a minute that Jared would be a great father. He was even tempered and logical, but he knew how to let loose and have fun.

"What makes you think Jared would be interested in parenting your child, Mercedes Ashton, uh, Maxwell?" she muttered.

He'd had the best wife on the planet. How could she measure up to a domestic goddess like Chloe? Her friend had been petite and motherly, kindhearted and generous. She'd had an amazing knack for decorating, incredible talent in the kitchen and a green thumb.

Mercedes stayed out of the vineyard for fear of killing the vines the way she'd killed every houseplant she'd ever been given. Puttering in the kitchen would never be her favorite activity, and she'd decorated her apartment all in the same shade of mocha so nothing would clash. Chloe had laughed and given her the quilt and other colorful items to brighten up the place.

Mercedes tended to speak her mind, whereas Chloe was more likely to be ladylike and polite. And Mercedes had already established that she was more selfish, driven and competitive than Chloe. They were so different it was a miracle the two of them had become friends.

No, Jared wouldn't be getting a bargain in her, but he would be getting a woman who would respect him for who he was and wouldn't try to change him.

She sipped from her water bottle and rechecked her watch. What was wrong with her? This wasn't her usual pregnancy icky feeling. Not that she'd been pregnant long enough to have a "usual," but she did feel more lethargic than she had over the past couple of weeks.

Branches snapped in the distance. She straightened. Please let that be Jared. And then his long-legged stride carried him into the open. Her heart hitched at the sight of his handsome mug. Morning stubble covered his strong jaw, and his eyes were as blue as the sky above. His snug black T-shirt revealed the depth of his pectorals and the breadth of his shoulders, and his snug, faded jeans accentuated long, muscular legs, a flat belly and the substantial male package in between. Her insides warmed at the memory of just how substantial.

Why had it taken her eleven years to notice Jared Maxwell had a killer body? In fact, her best friend was a certifiable hunk. Mercedes exhaled and shook her head. Thoughts like that were unnecessary and unwise.

Her relief in finding him didn't last long. His expression blanked as if he wasn't glad she'd tracked him down. She swallowed hard. If he apologized for last night she didn't know what she'd do.

Jared slowed when he spotted Mercedes sunning on a rock at the lake's edge. His pulse rate doubled. "What are you doing out here?"

"Looking for you." She rose slowly and dusted off the seat of the multipocketed hiking shorts he'd packed for her. He couldn't help wondering which bra and panty set her unisex outfit concealed. His heart hammered faster in memory of the sinful confections he'd found in her drawer.

The sun danced off her untamed curls and highlighted the spattering of freckles on her nose that she hadn't bothered to hide under makeup today—probably because he'd forgotten to pack her makeup. He'd also forgotten her hair toys, and for that he was glad. He liked her hair loose instead of scraped back into that twist thing she usually did.

"We usually hike together." Her cautious tone gave no clue to what she was thinking.

He gazed out over the mirror-smooth water. The gentle breeze barely disturbed the surface. All morning long he'd had a nagging suspicion that more than guilt had driven their love-making. Had last night been a pity lay because she felt sorry for him or a consolation lay because she'd needed reassurance that she was desirable after that jerk Bradford dumped her?

Did she feel he'd used her and betrayed her? Jared studied her neutral expression. "I needed some time to get my head together."

Or had last night been a result of the overactive hormones Mercedes had mentioned? Chloe's pregnancies had never affected her that way. As a matter of fact, once Chloe conceived she'd often pushed him away as if he'd done his job by making her pregnant, and she no longer needed him.

And Chloe had been shy in bed. She'd needed coaxing and TLC.

Mercedes, on the other hand— Heat blasted through his veins. He'd never made love as wildly as he and Mercedes had last night. He shoved a hand through his hair and cleared his throat. He only hoped she would forgive him for crossing the line. "Last night—"

"Was pretty amazing," she interrupted.

Her answer threw him off balance. He searched her face, and though his heart pounded like a jackhammer, his chest muscles constricted at the doubt clouding her eyes. Did she have regrets? "Yes."

"Who'd have thought you and I would be so…" She shrugged and looked away, clearly ill at ease.

Explosive. "Yeah."

Mercedes had been an aggressive lover. His need had been so great he'd been afraid he'd hurt her, and he'd tried to hold back, but each time she'd pushed him beyond the limits of his control.

Had he only been one more man in the line of revolving men in her life? Not that Mercedes was promiscuous. She was extremely selective in choosing the jerks with whom she became intimate. Jared could tick off the fools' names on one hand since she usually confided in him, once the guys had been shown the door.

And why did the thought of being just another one of Mercedes's lovers make him want to crawl out of his too-tight skin? He shoved the unpalatable thought aside.

Chloe had once claimed that Mercedes always chose men like her father, men who couldn't or wouldn't love her. He certainly fit that description. Sure, he loved Mercedes *as a friend,* but a strong, passionate woman like Mercedes deserved more than a man who'd proven he had feet of clay. She deserved a man who'd be devoted to her heart and soul. And his heart was no longer his to give.

He'd left her bed this morning because from the moment he'd awoken beside her he'd wanted to make love to her again. The hunger she'd unleashed in him exceeded anything in his experience, but last night shouldn't have happened and if she'd turned away in regret or cursed him…

He ground his teeth, snatched up a pebble and skipped it over the lake's surface. Anger and regrets were only what he expected.

"Jared, last night doesn't have to change anything between us."

His jaw dropped open. He snapped it shut and examined her earnest expression. How could last night not change everything? He'd betrayed Mercedes's friendship. A man didn't screw his best friend.

And then there was Chloe. He'd betrayed his wife. His first

wife. He'd always love Chloe, and he could never risk that kind of love for another woman. Not even Mercedes.

He'd made a mistake, but he didn't have any clue how to rectify the damage. During his hike he'd tried to analyze the situation and divide it into manageable parts, but setting an action plan defeated him. For only the second time in his existence—the first being after he'd lost Chloe and Dylan—he couldn't see a viable path ahead. He wasn't ready to cut Mercedes from his life, but he couldn't foresee their friendship returning to the previous comfortable footing.

He shook his head. "How can last night not change our relationship?"

She shifted on her feet and turned toward the water. "As long as neither one of us expects this to turn into hearts and flowers and romance, then we should be okay. Sex can be just one more physical activity we enjoy together like kayaking or rock climbing."

He rubbed the back of his neck. Should he be insulted? Was she trying to say what happened held no more significance to her than a weekend hobby? That didn't sound like Mercedes. "You're saying you'd settle for sex without love?"

She looked at him over her shoulder. Sadness and resignation filled her eyes. "I always do. Love complicates a relationship. Feelings get hurt. Hearts get broken."

Understanding clicked in his mind. Mercedes had been hurt by a jerk or two in college and by Spencer Ashton. She'd watched her sister's first marriage go from blissful to verbally and mentally abusive. "Love doesn't have to be that way, Mercedes."

Her brows leveled. "I'm not willing to risk it. Are you telling me you're ready to jump back into the dating pool?"

"No."

She tilted her head at what he'd come to recognize as Mercedes's I'm-ready-to-debate-this-all-week angle. "And are you willing to live without sex for the rest of your life?"

Last month that question would have been easy for Jared to answer. Yes, he could live without sex. He had for more than six years. But today, simply being near Mercedes aroused him. He vividly recalled her scent, her taste, the satiny texture of her skin and the hunger she'd imbued in him. His jeans tightened over his expanding flesh.

A knowing smile curved her wide mouth. "Weighing the pros and cons again, Jared?"

"I always do." He'd never been able to have casual sex with a woman for whom he felt nothing, and what Mercedes offered sounded too good to be true. He'd discovered that in most too-good-to-be-true cases there were hidden faults running beneath the surface.

She tipped back her head, revealing the tender underside of her neck and tempting him to agree just so he could kiss her again. "You're the one who suggested we tell the press that we were friends who became lovers."

"Mercedes, I don't know if sex between us is a good idea. Our friendship is too important."

"We trust each other, and we both know not to expect more than the other is able to give. Sex between us would be safe sex."

"I'll think about it." Hell, he probably wouldn't be able to think about anything else. "Ready to head back?"

"Sure." She turned quickly and he caught her wince.

"Is something wrong?"

She shrugged one shoulder. "I might have set too quick a pace on the way up here."

"That's not like you. You know your limits."

"You're right. I do. Let's go." She took off down the trail

and Jared followed. They'd made it about a quarter mile when he noticed the unevenness of her stride.

He picked up speed to draw alongside her. The narrowness of the trail meant their arms and shoulders bumped with each stride. "Mercedes, what's going on?"

She glanced at him but didn't slow her pace. He noticed the rigid set of her jaw and the pallor of her skin. "I think we might have overdone it last night. Either that or you're larger than I'm used to." She blew a stray curl off her forehead. "Well, that was definitely the case, but—"

His blood chilled. He ignored her flattery and grasped her bicep. "Did I hurt you?"

She stopped and faced him. "No. Never. I think we just had a little too much of a good thing. Sort of like eating an entire pint of ice cream after being on a strict diet."

He didn't buy her excuse. "If you won't tell me what the problem is, then I can't help you solve it."

She rubbed her lower abdomen. Worry clouded her eyes. "I'm having cramps."

His muscles locked. And his eyes tracked the movement of her hand on her belly as if hypnotized. Was she losing the baby? Dear God, had his loss of control last night caused her to miscarry? He scanned the steep hills around them. There wasn't anywhere to fly in a rescue team. He'd left his cell phone at the cabin because he knew from experience that he couldn't get a signal here. "I need to get you to a doctor."

She shook off his hand and trudged down the trail. "We're almost a mile away from the cabin. Let's see how I feel when we get there."

"You're going either way."

Her step hitched, but she didn't stop. "We're hours from my doctor in Sacramento."

"Then you'll have to go to the nearest emergency room."

"Great. Press." And then she sighed. "Okay, I can deal with the press."

Her acquiescence worried him more than an argument would have. "Can you make it to the cabin?"

"Sure." But her breezy answer lacked confidence.

"But?"

"But it hurts more when I walk, and the faster I go the worse it gets." Her reluctance in making the admission was clear.

He stopped her again and held out his backpack. "Put this on."

She looked at him like he'd lost his mind. "You want me to carry your pack?"

"Yeah, and then I'll carry you."

"I don't think—"

"Don't think. For once, Mercedes, could you do what I say without arguing?"

She stiffened. "Don't think sleeping together gives you the right to boss me around."

"I may have caused this, so would you shut up and get on my back."

"Isn't the phrase supposed to be shut up and get *off* my back?"

Her forced levity didn't make him laugh. "Aren't you worried about your baby?"

The shadows in her eyes darkened and her shoulders drooped. "Yes. I am."

"Then let's go." He turned his back and squatted.

After a hesitation, Mercedes climbed on and looped her arms around his neck. "This is crazy. I'm too heavy."

"It's not crazy if it keeps you and your baby safe, and you're a featherweight. I've carried packs heavier than you."

A slight exaggeration, but she didn't argue. Straightening, Jared hooked his arms under her legs and set off down the path. Adrenaline pumped through his veins lightening his load.

He couldn't live with himself if he hurt Mercedes or her baby. Hell, yes, he could, but he wouldn't like it. Whatever happened he'd be there for Mercedes. He owed her.

Eight

"Newlyweds, huh?" the young male E.R. technician asked Mercedes. A smile twitched on his lips. "How long have you been married?"

Was this freckle-faced boy old enough to be out of school?

Mercedes tried to smile back, but it was difficult to be friendly when fear had turned her face into a frozen mask. The ache in her belly hadn't relented, and when she'd gone to the bathroom before leaving the cabin she'd cried out at the knife-stabbing pain. The tech had made her repeat that torturous procedure here.

Was she losing her baby?

"We've been married a week. I haven't had time to get my license or insurance card switched to my new name, but the health insurance is valid."

"Hey, I believe you. The doctor will be in as soon as we get your lab results. Call me if you need anything." He left with a casual wave. If his smiles and relaxed attitude were designed to make her feel less afraid, they failed.

Mercedes searched Jared's grave face, and guilt swamped her for dragging him through this. Losing his own babies had been hard for him, and his obvious tension told her that he was reliving those memories today. Even though he hadn't said one negative word during the hike back to the cabin or the drive to the hospital, she knew he thought she was losing her baby. The worst part was she did, too.

A sob stalled in her throat. "You won't leave until we talk to the doctor?"

He clasped her hand. His jaw went rigid. "I'm not going anywhere."

"Thanks." She took comfort in his support and wished she wasn't such a coward.

"Would you like me to call your mother?"

"Not yet." What could she tell her except that she was scared out of her mind? Her mother didn't need that worry. Besides, if she spoke to her mother, Mercedes suspected she'd probably break down and cry. "Let's see what the doctor says first."

Jared massaged the back of his neck with his free hand. "Did that guy examine you while I was filling out the admissions forms?"

"No. He's only a technician. He took my vitals and had me pee in a cup. That's it. But you'd think he'd be a little more concerned." She tugged at the hospital gown, trying to cover her bare back.

"We should have driven to Sacramento." Jared rose and reeled back the curtain as the young man passed by their area. "Why haven't you examined her? She could be—" Jared glanced at her and then back to the tech "—her baby could be in trouble."

The guy grinned. *He actually grinned.* "Look, sir, relax. The doctor will examine your wife when he arrives, but you're newlyweds. Your wife has the classic symptoms of honeymoonitis."

"What?" she and Jared said simultaneously.

The tech tried and failed to control his amusement. Tilting his head, he whispered conspiratorially, "It's a bacterial infection of the bladder caused by frequent sex. Honeymooners are notorious for it."

Mercedes closed her gaping mouth. Her skin burned. "That's it? But what about my baby?"

"The doc will be here in a second. He'll cover all the bases." He left again.

Jared paced the small curtained cubicle like a caged animal. The minutes dragged by at a snail's pace. He pivoted at the end of her bed and pinned her with his gaze. "I don't like his attitude. He's too damned flippant. Honeymoonitis, my butt."

She clasped her hands over her belly. What would happen if she lost her baby? Would her marriage to Jared end? Would their friendship do the same? Neither course bore thinking about.

What seemed like an eon later, the curtain slid back and an older gentleman stepped in with a female nurse on his heels. "Mr. and Mrs. Maxwell, I'm Dr. Hicks, and this is Jan Reed, your nurse."

The doctor shook hands with both of them and then flipped through the chart before pulling the curtain closed. He did a thorough exam and peppered Mercedes with questions. She tried to pretend Jared wasn't standing right by her shoulder when she put her feet in the stirrups and the doctor got up close and personal. If she hadn't been terrified of the diagnosis she would be embarrassed.

When the doctor finished the exam he tossed his gloves in

the bin, washed his hands and wrote on the chart. He had a quiet discussion with the nurse, which Mercedes couldn't hear no matter how hard she strained, and then Jan departed. The doctor helped Mercedes to sit up. Each passing second seemed like a lifetime's delay, and Mercedes's nerves stretched until she wanted to scream.

Dr. Hicks observed her over the top of his half glasses. The older man's serious expression turned every one of Mercedes's muscles into stone. "Mrs. Maxwell, I suspect you have a urinary tract infection, a UTI. Normally, we'd write a prescription for antibiotics and send you home, but your pregnancy complicates the situation. The good news is your lack of fever leads me to believe you haven't progressed into a kidney infection yet."

A kidney infection? That sounded scary. Mercedes's stomach clenched. "Why is that good news?"

He regarded her solemnly. "I'm not going to sugarcoat this. A kidney infection could cause you to go into preterm labor, and ultimately, if we can't get the infection under control there's a risk of kidney failure, septic shock, respiratory failure and death."

Death! A chill of terror raced over her. She wasn't ready to die, and she didn't want to lose her baby, either. She cradled her stomach. Labor at eleven weeks. Her baby would never survive.

It wasn't until the nurse dropped a heated blanket over Mercedes's shoulders that she realized she was shivering.

Mercedes searched Jared's set and pale face. He stood rigidly beside the bed with his hands fisted by his side. "But I don't understand. I didn't have any symptoms until today. At least, I don't think I did."

The doctor nodded. "You're probably right. In most cases, a nonpregnant woman would notice the discomfort of a

UTI relatively early on, but pregnancy suppresses your immune system to allow your body to tolerate foreign matter, like a fetus, a placenta or even bacteria. A pregnant woman usually has a sudden onset of symptoms, as you did today.

"Treatment of an acute UTI is serious business. Our goal is to stop the infection before it progresses into your kidneys, and chances are good that we will since you're not allergic to any of the preferred antibiotics."

Chances are good. Mercedes hugged herself. "You mean I could still lose my baby?"

"Yes, Mrs. Maxwell, the risk factors are there, but I'm going to do my best to minimize them."

"How?" Jared asked in a strangled voice.

"I'll admit your wife to the hospital. We'll run a course of intravenous antibiotics and retest her tomorrow. If she responds to the treatment, then we'll probably let you take her home in a day or two with an oral prescription and a promise to follow up with her doctor."

"And if I'm not responding?" Mercedes asked, but she was very afraid she wouldn't like the answer.

"Then you'll be our guest for as long as it takes. We'll tackle it one day at a time and face each obstacle as it arrives."

Tension deepened the lines bracketing Jared's mouth, and worry and guilt clouded his eyes. She knew what he was thinking. He blamed himself. He'd said as much on the trail.

She'd hate for her night with Jared to become fodder for the press, but she'd rather live with the public airing of her private business than have Jared hold himself responsible if something happened to her or her baby.

"Doctor, the technician called this honeymoonitis, but we didn't…last night was the first time we, um, consummated our marriage. We couldn't have caused this, could we?"

The doctor's brows lowered. "No, Mrs. Maxwell, this isn't

honeymoon cystitis. As I explained, changes in a pregnant woman's body make it the perfect breeding ground for this type of bacteria. Your bacterial counts have probably been high for days, possibly even a week."

So Jared couldn't take the blame. "Thank you."

Dr. Hicks looked surprised by her gratitude, and then he glanced at Jared and nodded as if he'd dealt with nervous husbands before. "Any more questions?"

Mercedes bit her lip. "Yes. How will this affect my baby?"

He patted her hand and then stepped aside for the nurse to insert an IV. "Studies show you're very likely to have a normal pregnancy and a healthy baby if we can get past this stumbling block. I won't kid you. This is serious business, Mr. and Mrs. Maxwell, but you and your baby are in good hands here at Mercy Hospital. Give us an hour and we'll have you snug in a private room upstairs."

Finally some good news. It was about time.

The scent of antiseptic, the hustle of people and the cries of pain from a nearby cubicle dragged Jared under the depths of his memories as if he'd gone over the side of the Golden Gate Bridge with concrete blocks tied to his ankles.

Chloe and Dylan had died in an emergency room, and though this was a different E.R., it felt the same, smelled the same, sounded the same. And the stakes were just as high.

He could lose Mercedes.

Fear grabbed his gut and squeezed with an iron-clad grip as history bore down on him. Another night. Another wife. Another innocent baby. Gone.

His heart pounded, and sweat broke out on his upper lip. He endeavored to remain stoic for Mercedes's sake, but a heavy sense of helplessness weighed him down.

He couldn't fix this.

"You can call my mother now." Mercedes's quiet voice jerked him from his painful rumination.

He forced his stiff neck muscles into motion and shook his head. "I can't use my cell phone in here. I'd have to go outside to call, and I'm not leaving you."

As much as he wanted to run, he couldn't leave her here alone with her fears, and as much as he wanted to pull her into his arms, hold her tight and smooth her unruly curls, he wouldn't do that, either. He wasn't convinced last night hadn't been a mistake.

Mercedes worried her bottom lip with her teeth. "The press is bound to get wind of this since my driver's license is still in my maiden name. I'd prefer that my family hear about my hospitalization from us rather than from a reporter calling to ask them for details on a situation of which they're unaware."

"The doctor promised he'd have you in a bed upstairs within the hour. As soon as you're settled you can call your mother from the phone in your room. Hearing your voice will reassure her more than hearing mine."

"I guess you're right. Dr. Hicks sounds like he knows what he's talking about." The fear darkening her eyes contradicted her words.

Why did he get the impression Mercedes was trying to soothe him when it should be the other way around? He pulled up a stool, sat beside the bed and covered her hand—the one not tethered by the IV slowly dripping the potentially lifesaving antibiotics into her veins. "He does, but I'll call Dr. Evans later to be sure. If she has any doubts about your care here, then we'll have you transferred to her hospital by ambulance."

Jared laced his fingers through Mercedes's and said a silent prayer, something he hadn't done since his pleas had gone unanswered the night he'd lost Chloe and Dylan. He didn't want to lose Mercedes.

He loved her.

The knowledge hit him like a freight train at full speed. He hadn't seen the locomotive coming and now it was too late to step out of its path. The muscles in his chest constricted, and he couldn't draw a breath. Despite his vows to never love again after Chloe's and Dylan's deaths, somehow Mercedes had crept into his heart during the past five years.

He hoped Chloe could forgive him.

There was nowhere for Jared to hide in the confining curtained cubicle while he grappled with his discovery, his guilt and the realization that he and Mercedes didn't have a future together.

She'd married him solely to protect this child, and if she lost her baby she'd no longer need him. Even if she managed to get past this crisis, Mercedes liked men who made her laugh, men who could dance and schmooze at the cocktail parties her job with Louret Vineyards required. He wasn't that man. Not anymore. He'd learned to avoid affairs that required small talk with strangers, because folks invariably asked if he had a wife and kids. He knew they didn't mean anything by it. They were just trying to make conversation, but it was like a sneak attack every time and each time it left him reeling.

Could Mercedes be happy with a loner like him? Probably not. Their occasional escapes were one thing, but Mercedes wouldn't find a steady diet of isolation palatable for long. Besides, she liked variety. None of her men had lasted long before she found a reason to cut them loose.

And if she ever found out how weak he'd been after losing his wife and son, she'd lose all respect for him.

The painful knowledge that their relationship was doomed settled over him and filled him with resolve. He wanted Mercedes to be happy, and as soon as he got her out of here he planned to set the wheels in motion to ensure her happiness.

Mercedes jerked awake as the car slowed. Blinking her gritty eyes, she straightened in the seat and tried to banish the lingering sense of longing brought on by her dream about sharing a home with Jared and a houseful of dark-haired, blue-eyed children. Thoughts like that would get her in trouble.

"Why are we coming here?" Mercedes asked Jared as he drove up the long driveway of The Vines, her family's home and the scene of their farce of a marriage. He passed the left-hand turn that led to the winery and her office. Had she only been gone three days? It seemed much longer since she'd been strong-armed into a vacation. Some vacation.

"Your mother has agreed to take care of you while I'm out of town." Jared pulled his SUV to a stop in the circular drive in front of the entrance and cut the engine.

He was leaving and leaving her here? "You're going out of town? On a B&B buying trip?"

"No. I have personal business to attend to." His short tone warned her not to ask questions, and for once she didn't have the energy to challenge him.

What was she? A piece of damaged merchandise being returned to her original owner? "You can take me to the cottage. The doctor said it would be okay to resume my normal activities."

His expressionless gaze held hers. "Do you really want to risk being alone on your first day out of the hospital?"

Was being alone really the issue? Did he not want her in his cottage anymore? She didn't ask, because she was afraid she wouldn't like his answer. "I guess not. How long will you be gone?"

Jared's jaw remained tight. "Three or four days."

He exited the car and circled to her side. As soon as Mercedes's feet touched the ground, he startled her by sweeping her into his arms. She wound her arms around his neck and held on.

"I'm perfectly capable of walking," she protested, but surprisingly, she actually liked the warmth and security of being in his arms. His cologne teased her nose, reminding her of how he'd smelled when they'd been wrapped in the bed sheets and each other. Heat coiled in her abdomen.

"The doctor said for you to take it easy." He carried her toward the front door. His breath swept her lips with a hint of mint, tempting her to nibble that spot behind his ear that made him groan, but she didn't think the gesture would be welcomed.

During her stay in the hospital Jared hadn't touched her except to help her to the bathroom. Considering that she wouldn't have noticed the lack of contact a few weeks ago, she'd certainly missed it over the past two days. She yearned for the tangle and tug of his fingers in her hair, the moist heat of his mouth on her skin and the thick power of his body thrusting deep inside hers. She shivered.

Crazy hormones.

Her mother opened the front door as they approached and stepped onto the porch. "Nice drive?"

"She fell asleep the minute we hit the road and didn't awaken until we turned into the driveway," Jared answered before Mercedes could reply.

"I'm not surprised. Being in the hospital can be quite exhausting, but don't worry, Mercedes, you'll get plenty of rest here."

Jared followed her mother through the house and out into the walled garden where he set Mercedes down on a chaise and stepped away.

Her baby might be out of danger, but her relationship with Jared wasn't. Since leaving the cabin, Jared had built thick, impenetrable walls between them. The atmosphere remained strained and silent. And now she suspected he wanted her out of his house. The knowledge hurt.

He turned to her mother. "Caroline, thanks for agreeing to take care of Mercedes while I'm out of town."

"You know I'm always happy to have my children at home so that I can fuss over them."

"Will you call?" Mercedes hated that she sounded like a needy, whining wife.

Jared stayed silent for several moments. "If I can't make it home in time for your follow-up appointment on Wednesday afternoon I'll call to see what Dr. Evans has to say." He tucked a curl behind her ear and stroked a finger along her cheekbone. Mercedes's breath hitched and her pulse rate tripled. "Take care of yourself, Mercedes."

In her overly emotional state, the words sounded final, like a goodbye. Her eyes stung. "You, too."

And then he turned on his heel and left her. The quiet clang of the wrought-iron garden gate closing behind him drove a dagger through Mercedes's heart. His car engine started, and then the crunch of his tires on the drive faded in the distance. She lowered her head into her hands and clenched her teeth.

Would he come back? Or was this it? Was their marriage and friendship over? Pain crushed her chest.

A touch on her shoulder drew her gaze upward to her mother standing beside her chaise. "Are you ready for lunch?"

"No...not yet." Her baby was safe. Why wasn't she happy?

Because she wanted her old relationship with Jared back. She missed her best friend. Her bottom lip quivered. She bit it and ducked her head to hide the telling sign from her ea-gle-eyed mother. When Caroline sank down on the cushion beside Mercedes she knew she'd failed.

"What's wrong, Mercedes? Should I call Jared on his cell phone and ask him to come back? Are you in pain?"

Yes, but this wasn't the kind of hurt a pill could fix. "I think my illness reminded him too much of losing Chloe and Dylan."

Her mother brushed the hair off Mercedes's face. "I'm sure it's been difficult for him, but you and the baby are fine. In a few more months when you hold your son or daughter in your arms, you'll both forget all about this little setback."

Mercedes inhaled a shaky breath. Her throat burned as if she'd gulped scalding coffee. "I don't think Jared will be around for the baby's birth."

Her mother's brows rose. "Why would you say that? The man spent the last two nights in an uncomfortable hospital recliner because he refused to leave your bedside."

Panic and fear welled inside Mercedes. What if he didn't come back? She looked into her mother's understanding eyes and confessed. "This baby isn't Jared's."

Caroline wrapped her arm around Mercedes's shoulders and pulled her close. "I suspected as much, but I shouldn't have to remind you that it doesn't take biology to make a man a loving father. Lucas was a far better father to you than Spen-cer."

"I know, but Jared only married me because Craig's threat-ening to sue for custody. Jared's not in love with me."

Her mother waved a dismissive hand. "I've seen the way your husband looks at you. And that kiss at the wedding... You generated enough heat to wilt my roses. Don't try to tell me Jared doesn't love and desire you. The question is do you love him?"

Mercedes hesitated. She didn't want to tell her mother the

truth. Caroline already felt guilty about the horrible way
Spencer Ashton had treated her children. The recent discovery that they'd all been left out of Spencer's will had only
made her mother feel worse. The last thing Mercedes needed
to tell her mother was that because of Spencer she didn't ever plan to make the mistake of falling in love. "Of course I
love Jared, but he'll always love Chloe."

"And you think one chance at love is all we get in our life-
times? Surely my marriage to Lucas and Jillian's to Seth has
taught you differently."

"Yes, but…"

"Mercedes, I don't deny that I loved your father, and when
Spencer left me I thought my life was over. But it wasn't. I
picked up the pieces and moved on because my children depended on me. And then Lucas taught me to love again. It was
a very different love than my first, and I was wary because
I'd been hurt, but my feelings for Lucas were just as strong
as my feelings for Spencer." She paused and then shook her
head. "No, my love for Lucas is stronger because I trust him
implicitly—not because I'm young and naive and don't know
better, but because I knew him as a friend first and then grew
to love him later."

Caroline covered Mercedes's knotted hands. "The biggest
part of love is trust, and you've had trouble trusting the men
in your life. But you've always trusted Jared, and he trusts
you. Hold on to that now, Mercedes. Give him a chance to
prove you haven't misplaced your faith in him."

Caroline rose. "I'm going to get lunch, and I expect you
to eat it, young lady."

Hope unfurled in Mercedes's chest like a sail catching a
stiff breeze, but then the wind of optimism ebbed and hope
slackened. Doubts crowded in. Love wasn't in the cards for
her and Jared, but would he be willing to stay married and be

a father to Craig's baby? Not all men were as willing as her stepfather had been to take on another man's child.

How could she convince Jared that they belonged together as friends and as lovers? They liked and respected each other and, good heavens, they were good in bed.

Would that be enough?

Nine

Jared rapped once on the door to the upscale singles apartment Craig Bradford had moved into after leaving Mercedes and Napa. His briefcase seemed heavier than usual. It carried the weight of his future.

If he could convince Bradford to relinquish his parental rights, then Mercedes would be free of the threat to her baby and free to end their marriage. He wanted Mercedes to be happy, and that meant giving her the option of staying married because she wanted him in her life as her husband and her lover or going because she didn't.

If Bradford refused to sign the form, then Jared and Mercedes would stay married for the sake of her baby. He'd live with her and love her, but he'd never reveal his feelings because he couldn't bear to see pity in her eyes.

Jared rapped again with more force. Bradford's employer claimed Craig had left early for the day because he hadn't been well. Jared heard movement inside and a male voice cursing.

Seconds later Bradford yanked open the door. His clothes and hair were askew, but he didn't look sick, although he did look as if he might be pissed off and in pain. "What do you want, Maxwell?"

"To talk to you."

"I'm busy." Bradford tucked in his polo shirt and buckled his belt.

Jared noticed a fresh hickey on the man's neck and a smudge of red lipstick on his chin. Had he interrupted an afternoon nookie? Too bad. "This can't wait."

"Who is it?" a female voice called out from deep inside the apartment.

Bradford glanced over his shoulder and then scowled at Jared. "Come back later."

"Tell your girlfriend to get dressed. Is she your secretary?"

Red rose under Bradford's artificially tanned skin. "What's it to you?"

"Nothing if you don't mind me calling your employer to ask them if your secretary also took the afternoon off. And of course, I'd probably point out that you were fired from your job in Napa for sleeping with your secretary. Funny how you forgot to mention that to Mercedes. She thought you changed jobs to get away from her."

"Give me a minute." He shut the door in Jared's face.

Jared congratulated himself on doing his homework before driving south. The additional ammunition could only work to his advantage. Had Mercedes known Craig was being unfaithful during their relationship? No, Mercedes was into monogamy. She might not believe in long-term relationships, but she was loyal to the jerks she dated for as long as the affair lasted.

The door opened again. A busty brunette scooted past him

with her head down. She scampered down the stairs and out of sight. Bradford opened the door wider for Jared to enter. "Make it fast."

The black leather sofas and chrome and glass tables screamed bachelor with bucks. What had Mercedes seen in the jerk? Scratch that. He was a great salesman. Mercedes said he'd been helpful in wining and dining prospective clients for Louret Vineyards.

"What do you want?"

Jared narrowed his gaze on Bradford. "I want you to relinquish your paternal rights to Mercedes's baby."

"Screw you." Craig folded his arms and rocked back on his wingtip shoes with a smartass expression on his face. "What's the deal? You figured out the kid's not yours? Tell me something I don't know."

"You don't know whether Mercedes's baby is mine or not, and you won't know until after the child is born and a DNA test can be run. That'll cost you and so will the attorney you'll have to hire if you choose to fight for custody. I'm warning you now, Bradford, that as Mercedes's husband I'll expect you to cover your share of all costs incurred until the child turns eighteen—if he's yours—and you'll be expected to chip in for college tuition." A lie, but a necessary one.

Jared set his briefcase on the coffee table and opened it. He extracted a spreadsheet and handed it to Bradford. "As you can see from this projection, the cost of raising the average child on the West Coast and putting him through college runs roughly one million dollars. Divide that by twenty-two years, and you'll be expected to ante up a minimum for forty-five grand per year in child support."

Bradford wadded the paper and pitched it back into Jared's briefcase. "This is a load of crap."

"Wrong. I've done my research. Those numbers come

from a reputable child advocacy agency. You might be expecting Spencer Ashton's estate to cover those costs, but it won't. If the courts overturn the will, then the money and properties will revert to Caroline Lattimer Ashton Sheppard. Her children won't see a penny of that money until after her death unless she chooses otherwise. That's bad news for you for two reasons. One, Caroline hates you, and two, she's in excellent health. She'll probably live another twenty to thirty years. I don't see any Ashton money in your future with or without custody of Mercedes's baby."

"I spent nine months with Mercedes. She owes me palimony."

"Wrong again. Palimony is for unmarried couples who live together in an exclusive relationship. You and Mercedes didn't live together, and *you* sure as hell weren't exclusive.

"I've spoken to your previous secretary. She's pissed off at you for getting her fired, and she's willing to testify that you were unfaithful to Mercedes throughout the duration of your affair. And of course Mercedes's friends would also be willing to testify that you hit on them and made inappropriate remarks during the relationship.

"If you make the mistake of taking this to court then I guarantee Mercedes will countersue, and you'll end up owing her money for misleading her about your intentions."

Bradford muttered a string of curses and stalked to the window. "You expect me to walk away from my kid?"

Jared set his jaw. "Is it yours? You seemed to think it was mine three weeks ago."

"What do you expect me to think? Mercedes was fanatical about birth control, and your damned name came up in every conversation."

Surprise shot through Jared, warming him, giving him false hopes. He nixed the feelings and forced a casual shrug.

"What did *you* expect? Mercedes and I have known each other for eleven years. I've never been closer to anyone—not even my first wife."

He'd been bluffing, but as soon as Jared said the words he knew they were true. Mercedes knew him inside and out in a way that Chloe never had. Chloe had put him on a pedestal and ignored his weaknesses. Mercedes got in his face and made him confront the issues he'd rather avoid or kept him going until he found the strength to handle them. She'd taught him to be a survivor, to put one foot in front of the other and tackle one pain-filled day at a time. He couldn't have survived the past six years without her.

He'd never been a quitter. He hadn't given up when his father cut him off even though there had been plenty of days when it didn't look like his and Chloe's B&B would make it. It would have been easy to accept his father's loan offer, but instead Jared had sucked it up and worked ten times harder. He hadn't given up when his and Chloe's first and second pregnancies had ended in tragedy, and, thanks to Mercedes, he hadn't given up after losing wife and son.

Mercedes Ashton had made him a better man—*a stronger man*—than he'd been six years ago. Maybe he didn't have feet of clay after all.

"You're BS-ing me, Maxwell. You'd do anything for her."

"You're right. I would. Mercedes is my wife and I love her." Saying the words out loud for the first time filled Jared with a sense of rightness and renewed determination. He squared his shoulders and stared down at the shorter man. "Mess with her and you mess with me."

Bradford broke eye contact first. "Where can I get the damned form?"

Relief washed over Jared, but his job wasn't finished. He extracted the paperwork from his briefcase along with another copy of the estimated expense of raising a child. "Lucky for you, I had my attorney draw up the papers. Take it to yours and have him explain it word by word. I want you to know exactly what you're signing, because I don't want you crying foul later. I'll pick it up at your office Wednesday morning."

He shoved the batch of papers in Bradford's hand, snapped his briefcase closed and left the apartment with a combination of hope and dread in his chest.

Mercedes and his marriage were worth fighting for, and he'd just launched the first attack. But would this volley blow up in his face?

Would Mercedes stay? Or would she go?

Mercedes sipped her lemonade and fingered her cell phone as if touching it could make it ring. Jared had been gone for two days. The fact that he hadn't called and probably wouldn't be back in time for her doctor's appointment this afternoon or their Wednesday-night dinner bothered her far more than it should have.

Before she could rationalize her discomfort, the back door opened and Grant Ashton, Mercedes's oldest half brother and Spencer's firstborn son, stepped into the garden.

An interview Grant had happened to catch on TV had brought him to California eight months ago to search for the father he'd believed dead. He'd discovered his father alive and well and married to wife number three. Grant's arrival in Napa Valley had sparked off a series of disastrous revelations for the Ashtons.

Mercedes, her mother and siblings had been shocked to learn that Spencer had left a wife and two children behind in Nebraska forty-two years ago. He'd married Caroline Lattimer without bothering to divorce Grant's mother, thereby making Spencer's marriage to Caroline bigamy. Mercedes and her siblings had suddenly discovered they were illegitimate.

Grant's presence ought to make Mercedes uncomfortable, since one month ago Grant had been the chief suspect in her father's murder, but Grant's airtight alibi had cleared him, and his straightforward manner and genuine interest in uncovering the truth behind Spencer's lies made disliking Grant impossible.

"Hello, Grant."

"Feel like some company?"

"Pull up a chair." Mercedes looked into the same green eyes she saw in the mirror each morning—their father's eyes. She'd gotten to know Grant quite well. He'd been living at The Vines since January, but Mercedes hadn't seen him since Jared had dropped her off. She'd kept to her room and worried about where she'd go if Jared didn't come back for her.

Her apartment complex had a long waiting list, so returning to a larger one in the same complex was out of the question, and others in the area would be just as difficult to get into. She didn't make enough money to purchase a house on her own, and The Vines was overflowing with Ashtons from near and far due to her mother's gracious open-door policy. Mercedes wanted space for her and her baby to get to know each other without a lot of well-intentioned interference. She hoped Jared would be a part of those plans, but she was beginning to have her doubts. And that knowledge hurt more than it should.

A smile lit Grant's rugged face. "You look as if your stay in the hospital left you none the worse off. And congratulations on your pregnancy."

She grimaced. "Thanks. Word gets around, doesn't it?"

The papers had picked up the news of her hospitalization and broadcast it far and wide. Luckily, the intimate details of her night with Jared had been left out of the story. But she didn't want to discuss her precarious relationship with Jared or she'd lose her breakfast.

"Have you heard anything new about the investigation into Spencer's murder?"

Grant shook his head. "The detectives are still following the blackmail lead. Our father paid someone ten grand a month for at least a decade, and if they can figure out who was bold enough to bribe him, then we'll probably know who was bold enough to shoot him at point-blank range in his own office."

Mercedes couldn't help wondering if the hush money had been to cover up the secret of her father's marriage to Grant's mother or if another horrible secret would soon pounce on them unexpectedly. "So what's the news with your branch of the Ashton family tree? Have either Ford or Abigail heard from their mother?"

Grant's niece, Abigail, and his nephew, Ford, had also been her mother's guests at The Vines during the past nine months. It had been yet another surprise for Mercedes to suddenly find out she was an aunt to a twenty-four- and a twenty-six-year-old. Somehow she'd pictured herself bouncing her nieces and nephews on her knees and not having them arrive as fully grown adults.

Abigail had married Russ, Louret's foreman, in February, and the two of them had moved back to Nebraska for Abigail to open a veterinary practice. Last month Ford had married Kerry, her father's former executive assistant. What an insane year. There had been an Ashton marriage almost every month. How could Spencer's dishonesty bring happiness to so many?

Grant settled in a chair beside Mercedes. "We've had no word from Grace since she ran off with her salesman lover ten years ago. I'm trying to track her down. Before she disappeared, my sister liked being the center of attention, so if she's alive this media frenzy is bound to flush her out."

"I can't believe she'd abandon her children." Mercedes laid a protective hand over her baby. Dr. Evans had promised to do an ultrasound today. Mercedes couldn't wait to take a peek at her baby. She wished Jared were here to go with her.

Grant's lips twisted bitterly. "Like father, like daughter. My twin sister loved no one but herself."

Mercedes nodded. She couldn't believe there could be two people as heartless as Spencer Ashton in this world. He apparently hadn't loved any of the women he'd bedded.

Mercedes's heart skipped a beat and a chill raced down her spine. She hadn't loved any of her lovers, either. After getting her heart and ego severely dented in college, she'd deliberately chosen men she couldn't fall in love with, men who didn't have the power to devastate her the way her father had hurt her mother or the way Jillian's first husband had hurt her. Mercedes always warned her partners in advance that the connection would be temporary, and she entered relationships with an eye on the exit. She'd done the same with her marriage to Jared. They'd made plans to end the marriage even before they'd tied the knot.

She was her father's daughter.

Horrified, Mercedes clenched her fists until her nails dug into her palms. She'd hated Spencer because no matter how hard she'd tried to gain his approval, he couldn't love her, but was she any better than her father?

Was he too late? Jared hustled into the doctor's office and up to the counter.

The receptionist looked up. "Can I help you?"

"My wife, Mercedes Ash—Maxwell, had a three-o'clock appointment with Dr. Evans this afternoon. Is she still here?"

The woman checked the schedule on her desk. "She's with the doctor now. I'll take you back."

His heart pounded as he followed the woman through the rabbit warren of halls. Would Mercedes turn him away? And would today be the day she told him she wanted out of their marriage?

"Here we are." The blonde knocked on the door and poked her head inside. "Mr. Maxwell is here."

The door opened wider and Dr. Evans smiled in welcome. "Come in, Jared. We're about to take a look at your baby."

Take a look? His muscles locked. He forced them into motion and entered the room. Mercedes lay on her back on the examining table with a blue paper sheet covering her lower half. That drape meant she was bare under there.

He swallowed hard and dragged his gaze away from the blue paper and over the sage-green blouse she still wore to her face. He didn't see rejection in her expression, but he didn't see a welcome in her serious green eyes, either.

"You made it."

He jerked a nod. "Sorry I'm late."

A boxy machine with a viewing monitor stood on the floor beside the examining table. His stomach clenched. Dr. Evans pulled down the sheet to reveal the pale skin below Mercedes's navel. Not even Jared's tension could prevent the memory of pressing his face against the downy, soft area above a tangle of brown curls.

"This will be cold," Dr. Evans warned before she squirted clear gel on Mercedes's belly. She spread the gel with a device that looked like a shower head. "Jared, why don't you stand beside Mercedes's shoulder so you can see the screen? As I told Mercedes, the good news is the antibiotics have done their job. Her UTI has cleared up. We'll keep a close eye on her in the future to make sure it doesn't recur, but the important part is that it's unlikely to have affected the fetus."

His tension eased somewhat. Mercedes was out of danger. But Jared couldn't take his eyes off the ghostly black-and-white image on the screen. He'd been with Chloe during several ultrasounds. He knew what it meant when the doctor couldn't detect the blip of a heartbeat. He reached for Mercedes's hand and laced his fingers through hers. When he saw a little flash of white, he said a silent prayer of thanks.

Dr. Evans examined him with a knowing expression on her face. "There's your baby's heartbeat. You'll be glad to know that by the twelfth week the risk of miscarriage drops substantially, and Mercedes's nausea should also ease. As you can see, arms and legs have formed. Can you see the tiny fingers? I'm going to take a few measurements to make sure we're on target with your due date. Just sit back and enjoy the show."

The little shadow on the screen wiggled and took a recognizable form. Mercedes's baby. A lump formed in Jared's throat, and emotion welled in his chest.

He looked into Mercedes's happy, tear-filled eyes. He loved her, and she was going to have a baby. A fierce desire to be around for this child's birth and to give the baby a brother or sister filled Jared. Would Mercedes allow him to be a father to her child? Or would she take the document from Craig and run to the nearest attorney's office to file for a divorce?

"Do you want to peek and see if we can determine whether this is a girl or boy?" Dr. Evans asked. "It's early yet, but we can try."

Mercedes blinked and broke eye contact. She shook her head. "No. I want to be surprised."

Dr. Evans looked at Jared and waggled her brows with a teasing smile. "Do you want to know? We don't have to tell Mercedes."

He met Mercedes's gaze and squeezed her hand. "No. I don't want there to be secrets between us."

"Then I'll print out a few pictures of the little Maxwell for your scrapbook and let you two go. By the way, Jared, Mercedes told me about the honeymoonitis business. It's ridiculous, and you both need to know that sexual relations are perfectly safe. There are enough changes to adjust to during pregnancy without having to throw celibacy into the mix."

Him.

Mercedes.

Sex.

Less than three weeks ago the idea had shocked him. Today, the thought of making love to Mercedes elevated his blood pressure, his temperature and an insistent part of his anatomy. And then he remembered the forms he'd left in his car. He wanted to hold Mercedes in his arms, look into her eyes and make love to her one last time before handing over the document that made their marriage unnecessary.

He brushed a stray curl from her cheek and tucked it behind her ear before helping her to sit up. "That's good to know."

Mercedes's lips parted, and a flush climbed her cheeks. Desire flickered in her eyes, and Jared's heart knocked harder. Would she still desire him six hours from now? Six months? Six years?

Dr. Evans patted his shoulder. "I'll see you in three weeks." She left, closing the door behind her.

Mercedes crumpled the edge of the paper drape in her fingers and nibbled her bottom lip. "Should I move my things out of the cottage?"

He frowned. "No. Why?"

She shrugged and looked away. "You left me at The Vines. I thought maybe…"

I love you teetered on his tongue, but he held back. He

didn't want Mercedes to stay with him out of guilt or pity. She could make the decision to stay or go after he gave her the parental relinquishment form, and if she chose to stay, then he'd have the rest of his life to show her how much he'd come to love her over the past six years.

His gaze focused on her damp lips, but a doctor's office wasn't the place for the mind-numbing, doubt-blocking kiss he needed. Shoving his hands in his pockets, he stepped back. "I wanted you to be safe. Do you feel up to driving home or would you prefer to get a hotel room?"

"I want to go back to the cottage."

He tried not to get his hopes up, but it was hard. "I need to make a stop on the way home, and then I'll meet you there."

Mercedes nodded. "I'll get dinner."

Jared turned on his heel and left her. He needed to put the past to rest before he could take the next step in his battle for a future with Mercedes.

Ten

Mercedes sat in stunned silence after the exam room door closed behind Jared.

Evidently, she wasn't as heartless as her father after all, because her heart had been breaking ever since Jared had left her at The Vines. All she'd been able to think about over the past two days was what would she do without Jared? She'd been afraid she'd lost him, and the rush of happiness that had swept through her when he'd stepped into the examining room had put it all into perspective. There had been something in Jared's eyes that made her feel achy and tight, and this time she knew better than to blame those feelings on her crazy hormones. In fact, she suspected her pregnancy had only made her more attuned to the secret she'd been unwilling to acknowledge.

She'd fallen in love with her best friend. The knowledge both terrified and energized her.

How could it have happened when she'd tried so hard not to fall in love with *anyone?* When had it happened, and how could she not have recognized her feelings before now? When she looked back over the years since Chloe's death with hindsight, there were so many clues.

Mercedes always returned to Jared when her relationships ended. He soothed her wounded spirit and bolstered her damaged ego.

Why else could no man measure up to her high standards? Because she compared all her dates to Jared—the only man she knew who didn't register on her Twenty-Five Ways To Tell Your Man's a Loser list. And Jared was the only man she'd ever met who could make her forget the stress of her job and relax.

Her mother was right. Trust was a huge issue. Mercedes trusted Jared more than anyone else. Had she driven him away by throwing herself at him at the cabin and then by forcing him to face his worst nightmare—losing Chloe and Dylan—in the emergency room? She hoped his presence here today mean she hadn't.

Mercedes mechanically donned her clothes. Doubts continued to plague her. Had that night in the cabin meant anything to him at all or had he been without a lover for so long that any woman—*or even a knothole in a tree*—would have sufficed? She'd been hurting and she *had* thrown herself at him without really giving him an opportunity to say no.

Had he wanted to say no? The thought bothered her too much to contemplate. But his actions since that night gave little clue to his emotions.

Where did they go from here? Did she set him free? Did she beg him to stay? No, no begging. She didn't want his pity.

But if he stayed... She pressed a hand over her pounding heart. Marrying Jared had been a bigger mistake than she'd originally suspected, and destroying their friendship was the least of her worries. Without a doubt, Jared would break her heart. He still loved Chloe, and even if by some chance Mercedes could convince him to take a chance on loving her, staying married meant always taking second place to Chloe in his heart.

Not being good enough was a sore spot, since Mercedes had always come in second to her father's new family. Or was it third? Spencer had legally married the mothers of his first and third families.

Could she settle for being second best?

The lush green grass, towering shade trees, beautiful flowers hardly seemed like the right setting for heartache.

Jared stood in front of the small marble marker, and though sadness filled his heart, it wasn't the crippling emotion he'd once experienced. He could actually see a glimmer of light at the end of the dark tunnel in which he'd been living for the past six years.

He had been happy with Chloe, just Chloe, but she'd wanted a baby more than anything—more than him, he'd sometimes thought. It seemed fitting that she'd share her eternal resting place with their son.

Jared knelt to set the potted rosebush he'd brought with him at the base of the mother-and-child tombstone. The cemetery caretaker had promised to plant the bush tomorrow. Jared used to bring fresh flowers, but this plant would provide a steady supply of blooms in the future.

For years he'd thought he'd let Chloe down by failing to provide the houseful of children she'd wanted and by letting her get into the car and drive to her death. Jared had refused to accept the investigator's ruling that the wreck had been a freak accident despite the fact that the accident reports had revealed that the blown tire, which caused Chloe's vehicle to roll and crash into a tree, had been in good condition and properly inflated. Jared had wanted someone to pay for taking two innocent lives. For the past six years that someone had been him.

Hearing Mercedes try to take the blame had made one thing clear. Neither he nor Mercedes or even Chloe were at fault. Chloe and Dylan had been the victims of a tragic unforeseeable and unavoidable accident, and it was time he stopped beating himself up over it. It was time to move forward.

He sat back on his haunches. "I love her, Chloe. But you probably guessed that would happen. You said that I'd never have looked twice at you if I'd met Mercedes first, but you're wrong. You're both incredibly special women in very different ways. I'm lucky to have had each of you in my life."

He plucked a strand of grass and let it blow away in the breeze. "You asked me to look out for her if anything ever happened to you, and I'm here today to promise you that I'll be with her for as long as she'll let me. Mercedes needs me, even though she'd rather eat glass than admit it."

He rose and dusted off his hands. "I'll be back, but probably not as often. That doesn't mean I've forgotten you or Dylan. You'll always be here." He thumped his chest over his heart.

Jared withdrew a palm-size toy car that resembled his own SUV from his pocket and set it on the lip of the marker beneath Dylan's name. "You'll always be riding with me, son."

And then he turned his back on the past and took a step toward the future—a future he hoped to share with Mercedes and her child.

Mercedes lit the last candle and stepped back to view her handiwork. She hoped the table for two combined with dinner from Jared's favorite Mexican restaurant would set the scene for seduction. Anxious for his arrival, she walked to the window and peeked through the blinds. No Jared.

Craig and the men in her past had taught her a valuable lesson: sex without love didn't satisfy or fill the emptiness inside her. But making love with Jared had, even though she hadn't known she loved him at the time. She'd avoided falling in love because she hadn't wanted to be hurt, but she couldn't imagine anything hurting more than losing Jared.

No, she wasn't like her father. She'd rather love Jared and face the devastation of losing him than never experience love. Even if hers and Jared's relationship ended tonight, for once in her life she wanted to let down the walls she'd erected around her heart and make love knowing she loved her partner. But she'd keep her feelings to herself. She didn't want to make Jared uncomfortable. It wasn't his fault he couldn't love her back.

She glanced over her shoulder at the romantic table setting. She wanted it all; friendship and love, and she wanted it with Jared. Calculated risks like rock climbing and navigating white water didn't terrify her nearly as much as this simple dinner. But maybe one day Jared would be ready to love again, and Mercedes wanted to be the woman he chose.

The crunch of tires on gravel drew her attention to the driveway, and her heart leaped to her throat. Jared was home. She smoothed her hands over her pinned-up hair and met him at the front door, opening it before he could put his key in the lock.

He stopped on the welcome mat and his unblinking blue gaze locked with hers. Mercedes thought she might hyperventilate. She dampened her lips and studied his dear face. *She loved him.* "I picked up dinner at Casa Maria's."

"Smells good." He didn't make a move to come inside. Mercedes realized she was blocking the door. Heat climbed her cheeks and she moved out of the way.

He entered, set his briefcase on the sofa table, scanned the closed shades, the candlelit table and then appraised her. "Special occasion?"

Her mind went blank. Where was her usual lay-your-cards-on-the-table boldness? She knew what she wanted and how to ask for it, but for the life of her she couldn't blurt out that she wanted to make love with him because she was afraid he'd refuse. And then what would she do? "Um, no, I'm just happy to be home."

He shoved his hands in the pockets of his khaki slacks. "You were at home at The Vines."

She swallowed her rising panic. Was he going to ask her to leave? "You know I feel more comfortable with you than with my family. Besides, it's Wednesday. We belong together on Wednesday nights."

One corner of his lips twitched. "Only on Wednesdays?"

"I enjoy your company any day of the week." She silently groaned. How tepid. "Thank you for staying at the hospital with me. I know how difficult that must have been for you."

"I didn't like seeing you in pain."

She hated the awkwardness between them. "I meant—"

"I know what you meant, Mercedes, but your illness made me realize Chloe's death was a horrible accident. It wasn't my fault or yours."

"No, I guess you're right. I just wish…" What did she wish? If Chloe were still alive, then Mercedes wouldn't have discovered love, but she didn't wish her friend dead, either.

"The past can't be undone. We have to move forward," he said in a neutral tone.

The perfect opening… She reached deep for courage. "I'm glad to hear you say that, because I think we ought to try to make the most of our marriage."

His eyes narrowed. "In what way?"

"I want to be your friend…and your lover." She added the last in a rush.

His nostrils flared on a sharp breath. "Are you sure?"

Her heart fluttered like a hummingbird's wings. "Yes."

He closed the distance between them in two long strides and nudged up her chin with his knuckle. Mercedes held his gaze and reveled in the expansion of his pupils. Jared may not be in love with her, but he did desire her. "We're good together."

A smile trembled on her lips. "Oh, we're better than good."

Laughter sparked in his eyes. "You think?"

"I know. Let me show you." She lifted her arms and splayed her hands across his pale-blue button-down shirt. His heart beat steadily and rapidly beneath her right palm. Rising on tiptoe, she kissed him.

Jared encircled her waist and pulled her close, fusing their bodies together from shoulder to knee. The thin silk of her blouse and skirt were no barrier to the hard heat of his arousal against her belly. Mercedes gasped and Jared took advantage. His tongue teased hers, dancing, dueling, advancing and retreating until she wanted to groan.

She tangled her fingers in his short, springy hair. His mouth left hers to nip and suckle a trail of fire down her neck to the top button of her blouse. His hands swept from her waist to rest just below her breasts. Mercedes shifted on her feet as anticipation built in her belly. *Touch me,* she urged silently. He'd created magic with his fingertips that night in the cabin, and she wanted to grab his hands and lift them to cover her breasts for more of the same.

He lifted his head. "Are you hungry?"

She blinked? "What?"

"For dinner."

"Um, not really. I'd rather you kiss me again."

With a satisfied grunt, Jared swept her off her feet and carried her into his bedroom. Looping her arms around his neck, Mercedes rested her head on his shoulder. She loved being carried, and she couldn't remember anyone—not even her father—carrying her before Jared. He set her down beside the bed. As soon as her feet touched the floor, Mercedes yanked his shirttails from his trousers.

He caught her hands and threaded his fingers through hers. He kissed her knuckles and then lifted her hands to his shoulders. "Don't move your hands."

She struggled to regulate her breathing. "Why?"

"Because I want to take it slow this time."

Their night in the cabin had been hot and devastatingly sexy, but each time they'd made love it had been rushed—as if they'd each feared one of them would come to their senses at any moment.

Jared's plan to take it slow tonight was evident in every lingering touch and the slow sweep of his mouth and fingers over her skin. He unfastened the buttons of her blouse one at a time, beginning at the top. His lips trailed his fingers in a slow, seductive descent toward the waistband of her skirt. Mercedes's blood raced. He inched her blouse from beneath her skirt and over her shoulders. Her blouse fell to the floor. Jared traced the lacy edge of her bra with his tongue, and then he caught her nipple, lace and all, with his teeth. She moaned. With a flick of his fingers, the front fastening gave way and her bra joined her blouse on the floor.

He lifted her hands back to his shoulders, and then the wet heat of his mouth engulfed her swollen and highly sensitive flesh. Mercedes dug her fingers into his supple skin and held him close.

His muscles bunched and shifted as his hands roamed, hot, ardent and thorough over her. He stroked her back, her waist, her hips and thighs, sending waves of goose bumps over her skin. She trembled at the onslaught of sensation and at the urgency building in her womb. Her knees weakened and her impatience grew.

She wanted to look into his eyes as she held him deep inside her, knowing that she loved him. Determined to reach that goal as soon as possible, she reached for his shirt buttons.

"Not yet."

Jared released the button and zip on the back of her skirt, and the fabric floated to her ankles. He rubbed his cheek over the area below her navel. The light abrasion of his afternoon beard had to be the most erotic thing Mercedes had ever experienced. A quiver shook her. She cradled his head and threaded her fingers through his thick hair. His lips blazed a trail along the elastic waistband of her bikini panties.

He lifted his head and his passionate gaze meandered over her like a mountain trail traversing slopes and valleys. Her insides tightened with need.

"Turn around." His deep baritone voice sounded more gravelly than usual.

She frowned. "Why?"

"Just do it."

With any other man she would have refused. Because she trusted Jared, she turned, stepping out of her skirt at the same time.

"Put your hands on the bed."

She complied and her heart rate accelerated.

His rapid breaths steamed her skin as he kissed her nape and then each vertebra in a slow descent of her spine. He tugged her panties down her legs, and she stepped out of them. His hands caught her ankles, positioning them at the distance he desired and then his touch feathered upward light as a butterfly.

She jerked at the electrifying touch of his lips on her tattoo and then smiled. Jared liked her body art. The rose tattoo, once a reminder of love and loss, had become a sexy invitation—one she hoped he'd accept frequently.

"Why a rose?" His tongue outlined the flower and Mercedes's brain and her muscles turned to mush.

"Love is like a rose. Beautiful, but sooner or later you'll get jabbed by the thorns." Her voice faded when he kneaded her bottom and stroked between her legs with his long, talented fingers. She was wet and so hot. She wanted him to hurry.

Slowly he rose without putting an inch of space between them. His cold belt buckle scraped lightly and erotically over her buttocks until it rested against the small of her back. His strong arms encircled her, enabling him to cup and caress her breasts.

"You're beautiful." His rough whisper against the tendon of her neck made the fine hairs on her body stand on end.

His torso pressed her spine, spooning her as they stood by the bed. The contradiction of his hot body, the cool buttons of his shirt and the cold metal of his belt buckle made replying impossible. He pulled the pins from her French twist and dropped them on the table beside the bed, and then he buried his face in her hair. She leaned against him.

"I like your hair down." His breath warmed her neck and then his mouth opened over her fluttering pulse. He suckled and laved her while one of his hands parted her curls and found just the right spot to force a moan from her throat. "Like that?"

"Yes." Her breath came in shallow pants. The crest built swiftly—too swiftly. She wanted to look into his eyes when she climaxed, but he held her steady as release rippled over her, causing her to buck against the hard evidence of his arousal. He barely allowed her to rest before he brought her to the peak again. The second climax rushed upon her.

Mercedes reached behind her, wanting to touch him, too, but Jared lowered his hands and stepped away. She turned and found him removing his shirt with abrupt, jerky moves. "Let me help."

"I don't think I could handle your touch right now," he said through clenched teeth.

If it weren't for the tension in his face and the fire in his eyes, she would have been offended. Mercedes yanked back the covers and climbed into his bed. She turned on the bedside lamp and reclined on her side to enjoy the show. Last time they'd made love with nothing but moonlight. This time she wanted more. She wanted to see and taste every inch of the man she loved.

Jared opened his shirt to reveal firm pectorals and ridged abdominal muscles. His tiny brown nipples stood at attention. She'd seen his bare chest before, but this time was different. This time she knew she loved him. This time she knew she'd soon have him in her hands and inside her body. He kicked off his loafers and reached for his belt. Anticipation hummed in her veins.

She'd had no idea how arousing it could be to be in love with the man about to become her lover, and the way he looked at her as if visually feasting on her made her want to confess her feelings. But she couldn't do that.

He reached for his waistband.

"Wait," she stopped him. "Turn around and go slower."

A naughty grin curved his lips. "You want a show?"

"Yes."

He pivoted and eased his pants and boxers over his hips. She thought he might have added an extra wiggle or two for her benefit, and it didn't go unappreciated. She loved the contrast of the tanned skin of his back and legs against the paleness of his tight rear. Jared had a great butt: firm and round atop long, muscular thighs and a runner's well-developed calves. A fine coating of dark hair dusted all the delicious skin below his waist.

She scooted to the edge of the bed and knelt on the mattress. Mimicking the way he'd held her moments ago, she flattened her front against his back and reached around him to drag her nails across his hair-roughened torso. His muscles undulated beneath her light touch and his breath hitched. She sipped and nipped his neck, paying special attention to the spot behind his ear and relishing this man in a way she never had another.

Touching him, smelling him, tasting him brought her tremendous pleasure. Now she knew the difference between having sex and making love. This was so much more than what she'd had in the past. She wrapped her fingers around his thick erection and stroked him from the dense crop of curls to the tip of his shaft. She spread the slick dew over his silken flesh.

Groaning, he leaned back against her and allowed her touch for perhaps ten seconds, and then he grabbed her hand in one of his. He turned without releasing her, wrapped his free hand around her nape and covered her mouth with his. The force and passion of the kiss rocked her back on her heels. She loved knowing that she could break his iron control.

He banded his arms under her bottom, lifted her and carried her back onto the bed. He sprawled above her, pinning her to the mattress with the hard heat of his body. She wound her legs around his hips. Excitement made her breathless. Love and desire fueled her hunger.

She broke the kiss and met his gaze. "Love me, Jared."

With his ardent gaze locked on hers, Jared braced himself above her and then entered her with one long, slow thrust. A sound of sheer ecstasy bubbled from her throat as he filled her. He withdrew and returned, his tempo increasing with every lunge. Mercedes arched to meet him. She looked into Jared's blue eyes and cupped his beard-stubbled chin. Love welled in her chest.

Pressure built inside her until she thought she'd erupt like a shaken bottle of champagne. And then she did exactly that, bowing up off the bed as wave after wave of pleasure washed over her in a tingling spray. Her internal muscles clenched him, and Jared groaned her name and plunged one last time.

He collapsed to his elbows above her. Mercedes held him in her arms and relished his weight, the dampness of their skins and the harsh sound of their rasping breaths. She loved this man, and she wanted to spend the rest of her life with him. Was it possible? Could friends really become lovers? According to her mother and Lucas they could.

He eased to her side and pulled her head onto his shoulder. Somehow they'd ended up catty-cornered across his mattress. Their feet hung off the edge, and the blankets were wadded beneath them, making for a lumpy bed. As far as Mercedes was concerned, this was as close to heaven as she'd ever been.

Slowly Jared disengaged. He brushed a tangle of hair from her face and rose to stand beside the bed. Sadness edged the passion from his eyes, and a nerve ticked in his jaw. "I have something for you."

A tingle of apprehension climbed her spine at the gravity of his tone. "What?"

He held up a finger to indicate she wait and then disappeared into the den. Mercedes sat up and dragged the sheet over her nakedness. Why did she get the feeling she wasn't going to like this surprise?

Jared returned and handed her a flat manila envelope. The name of a law firm had been imprinted in the top left corner.

Her stomach knotted and she grew queasy. Her fingers trembled as she unfastened the brass clasp and reached inside to withdraw the stack of a half-dozen pages.

Nervously wetting her lips, she glanced at Jared, standing naked beside the bed. He nodded once, indicating she needed to read the forms, and then he reached for his pants. That telling cover-up sent her hopes of a future together plummeting.

She read the first paragraph and then the next. Disbelief warred with happiness in her chest. She quickly skimmed over the remaining pages. "Where did this come from?"

Jared's face remained expressionless, his eyes blanked, shutting her out. "I had my attorney's office draw it up. Bradford signed it when I reminded him that if he insisted on claiming paternity he'd be expected to pay child support."

Mercedes pressed a hand over her heart. She didn't know whether to cheer because she wouldn't have to battle Craig for her baby or to cry because her child had been rejected by its father, too.

She looked at Jared through misty eyes and her heart expanded. Only a man who loved her would go to this much trouble. "That's where you were the past two days?"

"Yes." His jaw muscles bunched. "We don't have to stay married now."

His quiet words hit her with the force of a full wine cask falling off the racks. Devastated, Mercedes gaped at him.

He *didn't* love her.

He wanted to end their marriage.

Then why had he made love to her with such tenderness? More *sayonara* sex? That's what had started her problem in the first place.

She'd thought her heart broken back in college, but she hadn't had a clue how badly real loving and losing hurt. Her chest squeezed tight, and her throat closed up. She couldn't breathe, and she thought she might faint. Her stomach revolted. Mercedes tossed the sheet and the documents aside and staggered to her feet. Pushing past Jared, she raced for the bathroom and barely made it in time to empty her stomach in the toilet.

When she finished being ill, Jared cupped her elbow and helped her to her feet. He dampened a washcloth, pushed back her hair and wiped her face. She snatched it from him, wiped her face and rinsed her mouth. Why did he pretend to care when he wanted her out of his house and out of his life? She snatched a towel off the rack and wound it over her nakedness.

Her world had ended. She'd gambled and lost. Her friend. Her lover. Her apartment. She'd been thrilled to discover she wasn't as coldhearted as her father. Now she wished she was, so she wouldn't have to endure this pain.

She shoved past him and headed to the den. He followed. Her nails bit into her palms as she turned to face him. "Are you asking for a divorce?"

"I'm offering you your freedom if you want it." The pain in his eyes and the raspy edge to his voice confused her. Was this as hard for him as it was for her? Was the legal legwork nothing more than a gesture of friendship? Or had he confronted Craig because he loved her?

She lifted her chin. "And if I don't want my freedom?"

His Adam's apple bobbed as he swallowed. "Then you need to know what you're getting." He looked away, took a deep breath and then met her gaze again. "I'm not as strong as you think I am, and we both know you don't respect weak men. After Chloe and Dylan died I wanted to die, too. I considered it."

Panic squeezed her chest. She could have lost him. "Jared, you're one of the strongest people I know to have been through the trials you've faced and kept going." She laid a hand on his arm. "I couldn't have stood losing you, too."

He covered her hand with his. "I know. And it was your voice that kept me from taking that last step—that and my promise to Chloe."

Mercedes frowned. "What promise?"

"To look out for you."

A surprised burst of laughter escaped. "Chloe made me make the same promise—to look after you if something happened to her." She clenched her fists and then asked because she had to know. "Is your promise to Chloe the only reason you allowed me to remain a part of your life?"

He hesitated. "No, Mercedes, you challenged me. You made me face each day. When I said I couldn't run the inn without Chloe, you're the one who suggested I find other couples that shared Chloe's dream but couldn't afford to live it. The idea of buying up failing B&Bs and hiring husband-and-wife teams to run them was yours. You even helped me find the financial backing to get the process started. You gave me a purpose for going on."

He lifted a hand and stroked her cheek. "And you let me remember, even though I know it hurt you to talk about Chloe, too. You'd known her a lot longer than I had."

She captured his hand and held it against her face. "Chloe brought us together and she kept us together. She was my best friend. Now you are. I don't want to lose that, Jared. You're too important to me."

She'd always thrived on challenges, but challenges came with risks. Should she play it safe or risk it all? All her life she'd avoided love to evade rejection, but if she didn't open her heart, then Jared could walk out of her life.

Releasing his hand, Mercedes braced herself. "If you want a divorce then I won't fight you, but there's something you need to know first. I love you, and not just as a friend. I'm *in love* with you, Jared."

Saying the words felt good, cathartic, but at the same time she teetered on a knife edge of tension. Her stomach knotted when he closed his eyes and exhaled a long, slow breath. She rushed on. "I don't know how it happened or when, and if you don't feel the same way, that's okay. I know I'm not Chloe. I'm not as loving or generous as she was. And I—"

His lids lifted and the emotion in his bright-blue eyes choked off her words.

"You don't need to be Chloe. You're perfect exactly as you are. And from where I'm standing you are the most generous woman I've ever met. You've devoted yourself to your family and to me. You've given unstintingly of your time and expertise in helping me find and promote the inns. You helped me rebuild not only my business but my life.

"I'm a number cruncher not a people person. I never could have done it without you. You have an uncanny eye for choosing exactly the right couples to run each inn. You help me make those peoples' dreams come true, and you gave me back my pride by keeping me from having to return to my father's company as a failure."

"I think you're underestimating your own strength and business savvy."

He threaded his fingers through her tangled hair and tipped her chin until only inches separated their mouths. Their gazes locked, and the passion in his eyes stole her breath. "I'm a stronger man and a better one for having known you. I love you too, Mercedes."

Hope and happiness filled her. Tears pricked her eyes, and a smile trembled on her lips. Her friend. Her lover. Her husband. Maybe they could have a future together after all.

Jared's brows dipped, and Mercedes tensed. "But I'm not like your other men. I'm not a charmer or a smooth talker."

Her muscles unknotted, and a wry smile twisted her lips.

"Thank goodness. As you said, I have a habit of picking out losers. I spent my entire life trying to earn my father's love. I think I must have subconsciously chosen men exactly like Spencer—men I knew I couldn't love and who were guaranteed to let me down. You, on the other hand, have always been my rock, and you keep me sane."

Mercedes worried her bottom lip with her teeth. "But I'm carrying Craig's baby, and I don't want my baby to feel unwanted or unloved. Not all men want to be a father to someone else's child, and I can understand if you don't."

Jared kissed her tenderly and stroked his hand over her belly. Heat settled beneath his palm. "I'll love your baby because it's a part of you, and the way I see it, he or she brought us together. I look forward to being a father to this child and any others that we might have together."

Mercedes had never wanted a houseful of children, so why did the thought of a crowded dinner table, sibling rivalry and the hectic mornings of her own childhood fill her with longing? "I'd like that, but if it doesn't happen…"

"If it doesn't happen we still have each other and this little tyke. Make a life with me, Mercedes."

A happy tear rolled down her cheek. "I can't think of anything I'd rather do than spend the rest of my days as your friend and your lover."

"Not just my lover…my love." And then Jared lowered his head and kissed her.

Mercedes rose on her tiptoes to meet him halfway.

Epilogue

"If you'd tell me where we're going once in a while I wouldn't have to pack so much," Mercedes said a week later as she squinted through the sunshine at the stately brick house ahead of them. "This doesn't look like a B&B."

"It's not." Jared glanced at her. She noted the apprehension darkening his eyes and tightening his jaw. Come to think of it, he had been unusually quiet during the drive. "It's my father's house."

Mercedes's breath hitched. "Is he expecting us?"

"I called and asked if he wanted to meet my wife. He said yes." He put the car in Park in front of the wide semicircular brick porch and turned in his seat. "You were right. My father may show his love in a different way, but he does love my brothers and me. I want to mend fences."

Mercedes cupped his jaw. "I'm glad you realized that before it was too late."

The front door opened and a man stepped outside. Mercedes stared, knowing Jared would look very much like this tall and handsome silver-haired gentleman in thirty or so years. She looked forward to being by Jared's side at that time. Perhaps they could retire to his cabin by the lake.

Mercedes pushed open her car door and met Jared in front of the vehicle. She laced her fingers through his and climbed the shallow steps beside him. His father's eyes—the same intense blue as Jared's—hungrily absorbed the details of the son he hadn't seen in years, and then his arms opened.

Jared hesitated. Mercedes was about to shove Jared forward when he moved into his father's arms of his own accord. The two men hugged. Tears rolled freely down Mercedes's cheeks. Damned pregnancy hormones. But she was smiling as she dug in her purse for a tissue to dry her face.

As Mercedes observed the reunion, she realized that if Craig ever asked to be a positive part of their baby's life, then she wouldn't keep them apart. Sadly, she didn't expect to have to make that decision.

Jared turned and extended his hand to Mercedes. "Dad, I'd like you to meet my wife, Mercedes."

Mr. Maxwell shook her hand and kissed her cheek. "I believe I have you to thank for today's visit, and for that I'm forever grateful. Thank you, Mercedes, for bringing my son home."

* * * * *

Look for the next installment of
DYNASTIES: THE ASHTONS,
Roxanne St. Clare's THE HIGHEST BIDDER,
available in October from Silhouette Desire.

Available this October from

DANGER BECOMES YOU

(Silhouette Desire #1682)

by Annette Broadrick

Another compelling story featuring

Brothers bound by blood
and the land they love.

Jase Crenshaw was desperate for
solitude, so imagine his shock when his
secluded mountain cabin was invaded
by a woman just as desperate—but only
Jase could provide help.

Available wherever Silhouette Books are sold.